The tall figure of a man landed on the tracks in front of them. "Let her go."

The voice was strong, deep and dark, with the barely concealed hint of a growl. Katie couldn't see his face.

The tall man lunged at her kidnapper, yanking him off her so suddenly the boy yelped in surprise, as he was tossed beside the tracks like a sack of bones.

Strong arms reached down toward her. Hands clasped her arms in a motion firm yet surprisingly gentle. "Hey. Are you okay?" She nodded as he used his strength to pull her shaking body to its feet.

"I'm fine, Mr...?"

"Mark. Mark Armor."

She stuck out her hand for a handshake. A curious smile curved up at the corner of his lips.

Come on, Katie, get ahold of yourself. It's not like you can just count on a handsome stranger to step in and save you.

MAGGIE K. BLACK

is an award-winning journalist and romantic suspense author. Her writing career has taken her around the globe, and into the lives of countless grassroots heroes and heroines, who are faithfully changing lives and serving others in their own communities. Whether flying in an ultralight over the plains of Africa, riding a camel past the pyramids in Egypt or walking along the Seine in Paris, Maggie finds herself drawn time and again to the everyday people behind her adventures, and seeing how we are all touched by the same issues of faith, family and community.

She has lived in the American South and Midwest, as well as overseas. She currently makes her home in Canada, where her husband teaches history at a local high school. After walking her two beautiful princesses to school, she either curls up on the couch to write, with the help of her small but mighty dog, or heads to her local coffee shop. She is thankful to her readers for allowing her to turn the adventures, and people who have inspired her, into fresh stories that made her pulse race and her heart soar.

KILLER ASSIGNMENT

MAGGIE K. BLACK

HARLEQUIN® LOVE INSPIRED® SUSPENSE

Recycling programs
for this product may
not exist in your area.

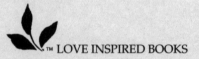

™ LOVE INSPIRED BOOKS

ISBN-13: 978-0-373-67576-0

KILLER ASSIGNMENT

www.LoveInspiredBooks.com

Printed in U.S.A.

Where can I go from your spirit?
Where can I flee from your presence?
—*Psalms* 139:7

With thanks to:
Paul for giving me the idea
Tammy and Blythe for helping it grow
and Jason for giving it wings

ONE

Katie Todd tightened her grip on the handle of her suitcase and tried to pretend she didn't know she was being watched. The sun had set long before her train had dropped off its few remaining passengers in Cobalt. Now damp, dark air hung over the tiny northern Ontario town, thick with the threat of rain. Behind her back, the lake spread out as still as a shadow. The small station was deserted except for one lone figure, lounging against a lamppost.

The young man had boarded the same train as she did in Toronto. He was in his late teens—twenty at most—and had sat there, hunched in the corner with his hands plunged deep into the pockets of a shapeless gray sweatshirt. When the conductor had announced, a couple of hours into their journey, that the train would be going out of service in the small town of Cobalt due to a rockslide on the tracks ahead, most passengers had opted to get off in the larger city of North Bay to either catch a replacement bus or find a hotel for the night. Only a handful of people had ridden the train to its final stop. Then, as the other passengers disappeared up the hill toward the gray shapes of town, the young man had stayed behind. His sharp eyes peered at her from underneath the brim of a baseball cap. They followed her as she moved. Katie shivered. Where was her taxi?

She never should have trusted Ethan Randall. When she'd managed to reach her boss at *Impact News* to warn him she was going to be delayed in reaching her assignment, the editor had insisted she take the train all the way to the end of the line, promising the newspaper would arrange transportation from there. Then her cell phone reception had dropped out, cutting off the call before she could even argue. She hadn't been able to get a signal back since.

Chances were Ethan hadn't even been listening. But you didn't last long at *Impact* if you didn't go where you were told. To call his management style chaotic was an understatement. The self-centered playboy didn't plan so much as react—changing assignments on a whim and then yelling at his staff for struggling to catch up.

This weekend was a perfect example. Here she'd been planning on getting her hands dirty at a fall cleanup event in Toronto's Don Valley. Instead, he'd sent her up north to cover the weekend gala that real estate developer Jonah Shields was holding on his

private estate. Shields was exactly the kind of irresponsible businessman she'd become a journalist to
expose. Now here she was expected to write some ridiculous fluff piece about how lovely his party was.

If all went according to plan, Ethan wouldn't be
her boss much longer. But if she wanted to keep her
job long enough to scoop his job out from under
him, she couldn't afford to mess up a single assignment. Even if the taxi he'd promised to arrange was
nowhere to be seen. She tried her cell phone again.
Still no signal. Probably because he'd changed their
work phones recently, and their new service provider
had no coverage this far north.

So, no taxi. No phone. Just a dark, empty train
platform growing colder by the second and a stranger's threatening glare. She took a deep breath and
ran both hands through long, blond hair, the color
of pure honey. Okay. She'd sort it out somehow. She
always did.

The tiny town lay dark and silent ahead of her,
barely more than a smattering of buildings, framed
by the shadow of the old mine. Surely there would
be something open in town and someone who'd let
her use a phone. She extended the handle of her suitcase and started across the parking lot. The young
man followed.

There was the sound of tires screeching. A white
delivery van was speeding toward the station. It
swerved into the parking lot and stopped short in

front of her. She jumped back. The man behind the wheel was huge, with a camouflage jacket and the grim, scarred face of someone who'd been in more than his fair share of fights. "Katie Todd?"

A cold shiver shot up the base of her spine. But she forced a polite smile onto her face. "Yes?"

"I'm Al. I'm here to pick you up." There was no company name on the van and no windows in the back, either. The bottom of the chassis was pock-marked with rust, and the whole thing stunk of fuel. Whatever this van was used for delivering, it sure wasn't people.

"I'm afraid there's been some kind of mix-up," she said. "I was waiting for a taxi."

Al smirked. "Hop in." Something cold and dark flickered in the back of his eyes. "I'll take you where you need to go."

The van didn't even have a license plate. No way even Ethan could've messed things up this badly. She stepped back and nearly bumped into the teen-ager who'd followed her from the train.

"Hey, Billy!" Al waved a big hand toward the kid. "How about you open a door for Ms. Todd?"

Billy snickered.

She slid both hands onto the handle of her suitcase and tightened her grip. "Thanks. But I feel like a walk."

Al's grin faded. He nodded to Billy. "Grab her." He threw the van's back door open. For a second, she caught a glimpse of a bare, empty space with a blanket and roll of duct tape on the floor.

Billy lunged. She swung her suitcase around hard with both hands, then let go, launching twenty pounds of laptop and clothes directly into the teenager's chest. He stumbled back. She ran, expecting any moment to feel hands grabbing her, pulling her back. For a second, she started up the road toward town. But when she heard the van's engine turn over, she swerved right and dove down the grassy hill toward the railway tracks. She'd never be able to outrun them on the road. But if she made it as far as the train tracks they'd be forced to chase her on foot.

Her feet slipped on wet fall leaves. She hit the tracks and pitched forward, falling onto her hands and knees. Billy was slithering down the hill behind her. Katie gasped for breath, stumbled to her feet and forced herself to sprint.

The tracks lay ahead of her, disappearing into the blackness, between ragged cliffs on her left and the lake to her right. She could hear Billy's footsteps pounding down the tracks behind her now. She didn't risk looking back. Didn't dare slow. Couldn't let herself wonder why someone would try to kidnap her. Or what they'd do to her if she were caught.

A light flickered on the cliffside in front of her. Then the small beam swung across her path, like someone waving a flashlight.

She hesitated. Billy leaped on her from behind,

grabbing her around the knees. He forced her to the ground, pressing her body into the railway slats. She screamed. His hands clamped around her ankles. He dragged her backward down the tracks. Her hands clutched desperately at the rails.

"Hey!" a male voice shouted. "Leave her alone!" Someone was scrambling down the cliff.

Billy's hand snapped to the back of her neck. Skinny fingers clenched the soft skin at the sides of her throat. "Don't move," he barked in her ear. "Or I'll kill you."

The tall figure of a man landed on the tracks in front of them. "Let her go." The voice was strong, deep and dark with the barely concealed hint of a growl. She couldn't see his face.

Billy knelt up, his hand remaining firmly clenched on her neck. A bony knee pressed into the small of her back. The weight of his body forced the air from her lungs. "Back off! I've got a gun, and I'm not afraid to use it." The tremor in his voice made her suspect he was lying, but when she tried to speak, she couldn't manage more than a whimper. "This is between me and her. Just turn around, walk away and pretend you didn't see a thing."

"I'm afraid I can't do that." He lunged at Billy, yanking him off her so suddenly the boy yelped in surprise as he was tossed beside the tracks like a sack of bones.

Strong arms reached down toward her. Hands

clasped her arms in a motion firm yet surprisingly gentle. "Hey. Are you okay?" She nodded, using his strength to pull her shaking body to its feet.

The crack of a gunshot split the night air. Billy had fired wildly, the bullet flying off into the darkness beyond. In a heartbeat, her rescuer threw himself between her and Billy, shielding her with his body. But all that followed was the click of Billy's gun jamming. The teenager swore. He scrambled to his feet and ran back down the railway tracks.

The man sighed. "Nothing more stupid than a novice waving a gun around. They pretty much never hit what they're aiming at." He unclipped a flashlight from his belt and switched it on. Light brushed along the stubble of his jawline. He was tall, with well-worn jeans and the kind of sturdy shoulders that implied their owner was more at home in a thick and wild forest than inside the walls of an office cubicle.

"If he had a gun, why not pull it out earlier?" She was relieved to feel her reporter's instincts kicking in. As long as she focused on asking questions, she'd be able to stay in control of her emotions.

"My guess is he wanted to take you alive."

Her knees buckled. She glanced past him down the tracks, the desire to run as far as she could from the terror behind her battled with legs that threatened to crumble beneath her. For a moment, she fought the urge to let herself fall into his arms and cry. But instead, she planted her feet firmly beneath her. They were still alone, at night, caught in the dark empty space between a cliffside and a lake. Hardly the time and place to let herself fall apart. Besides, this man could be anybody.

"What happened?" His fingers brushed along her arm. "Are you hurt?"

"I'm fine. Thank you. I just arrived at the train station, and two strangers tried to force me into a van."

She swallowed hard and forced her legs to walk, slowly at first, but knowing that each step would take them farther away from the men who had tried to kidnap her. "Where did you even come from?"

He matched his pace to hers. "There's a path that cuts down the cliffside. I was sitting on a ledge half-way up when I heard you scream."

"Alone? In the dark?"

He blinked. "I was testing some broadcast equipment. I'm an engineer of sorts, and broadcasting a radio signal off cliffs like these over still water are pretty much ideal conditions for testing signal strength. I just thank God that I decided to do it when and where I did." He said the last bit with a bit more emphasis than she was used to. His hand hovered just behind her shoulders, just enough to let her know that his arm was there in case she wanted the support. "But are you sure you're okay?"

She paused long enough to let her gaze meet his.

The lines of his face were tough and unflinching, which belied a more tender mouth than she was expecting. But it was the depth of concern reflected in his deep eyes that almost made her legs give way. She stepped away from his outstretched arm. He slid his hands into his pocket. "I'm fine, Mr....?"

"Mark. Mark Armor."

"Thank you for your help, Mark." Her voice sounded more formal than she'd been intending. But it wouldn't hurt him to realize she was hardly some damsel in distress. Last thing she wanted was another man thinking he could save her. "I'm Katie Todd."

She stuck out her hand for a handshake. A curious smile curved up at the corner of his lips. But he took her hand and shook it up and down firmly. Then his fingers lingered over hers. *Come on, Katie. Get hold of yourself. It's not like you can just count on a handsome stranger to step in and save you.*

"The priority right now is reporting this to the police." She pulled her hand away. "Obviously, the sooner I make a report, the better. But the last I checked I couldn't get a cell phone signal. Do you know where I can find a phone?" There was that smile again on Mark's lips. Like he couldn't figure out whether to be amused or impressed.

"Most cell providers have no coverage this far north. Here, you can use my phone."

Mark reached into his pocket and pulled out an

awkwardly shaped silver device that looked like a cross between a smart phone and a Smith & Wesson revolver. Katie ran her gaze all the way from the depth of his eyes down to the mud on his leather boots. Right, so well-worn jeans and a high-tech phone and he was testing broadcast equipment after dark in the middle of nowhere. Oh, right, and he wasn't the least bit fazed by being shot at. What was wrong with this picture? "That's actually a phone? I've never seen anything like it."

"I built it."

"You can actually get a signal with it here?"

"It's a satellite phone. The signal bounces off a satellite in orbit instead of using cell towers. I can get a signal pretty much anywhere in the world with it, no matter how distant or remote." Something in the way he said it made her think that he'd actually tried. "Is there anyone else we should be contacting? Were you traveling with anyone? Or was there someone who was supposed to be meeting you?"

"I'm just up here for work." On a nonsense assignment that was quickly unraveling before it even started. "I'm a reporter for a newspaper in Toronto." And hopefully its editor soon, once she managed to get Ethan out of the way. "How about you? I'm guessing from your gear you're with some kind of secret international law enforcement?"

Mark laughed. "Hardly. I run a small disaster-relief charity called Technical Response United

Solution Teams—or TRUST for short. We travel around the world helping local charities respond to humanitarian crises and disasters mostly by designing and building different gadgets and equipment to help them."

Disaster relief. Perfect. She took the phone and dialed 911.

Mark paced in front of the police station. After he'd given his statement, the officers had told him he was free to leave or welcome to wait for Katie. But the idea of being stuck in a chair in some waiting room gave him cabin fever—and there was no way he was about to leave.

Then again, why not just go? This was hardly the first time he'd come across someone in trouble. The way he'd always seen it, it was his responsibility to get that person to the right authorities. After that, he moved on.

So why wasn't he moving? Thunder rumbled in the distance. The smell of impending rain lingered in the air. Katie's face filled his mind. He remembered the courage and strength that had flashed in her dark brown eyes. The aching beauty of her smile, as she'd battled the tremble of fear in her lower lip. Not that she'd probably like him thinking about her as either beautiful or vulnerable. She'd practically shaken off the attack like she was even more afraid of showing weakness.

Now she was on the other side of a closed door, and it was taking all his self-control not to just walk back into the station and see if there was something he could do. He sent some hurried prayers for patience up toward the heavens. But the answer seemed in no hurry to arrive.

"Sometimes, all God calls you to do, is wait...." The voice of his buddy Zack flickered in the back of his mind. Part of an elite peacekeeping squadron, Zack often said the greatest strength came from self-control. It was still two days before they were supposed to meet up at the campsite, but he dialed his number anyway and left a quick message, asking him to pray for Katie. There, now he wasn't praying alone.

He looked back up at the sky, and a thought simmered in the back of his mind. Should he have asked Zack to pray for him, too? After all, tomorrow he was walking into a meeting with the one man he'd sworn he'd never speak to again—his father. No, the less said about that the better. Some battles were just easier faced alone.

He checked his watch. While he was at it, he might as well put a call in to Nick, his second in command at TRUST. Although, hopefully Nick had left work by now. It was hardly a secret Nick's fiancée, Jenny, was getting tired of finding him hunched beside Mark at the workbench long into the night.

Nick answered on the first ring. "Good to see you're still alive."

"Sorry. I decided to stop by the lake to run a quick broadcast test with the radio unit prototype—" and to ask God to give him the strength he'd need to face his dad tomorrow "—and I interrupted a crime in process."

Nick sucked in a breath. "Everyone okay?"

"Yeah. A couple of guys tried to abduct a woman as she got off the train. She's all right now. Just a bit shaken up."

"Thank God. When I see Jenny, we'll be sure to send up a prayer."

Guess that answered the question of whether he was still working. "You about ready to pack up for the night?"

"Pretty much. Jenny's on her way over. We're meeting with our pastor tonight to talk about something wedding related. I don't know what. But Jenny sounded pretty serious."

Mark ran his hand over the back of his neck. "Everything okay there?"

"I hope so." Nick chuckled nervously. "The bigger problem is we got a call from the Chipe Orphanage in Zimbabwe today. Their electricity is on the fritz due to flooding, and they were hoping TRUST could help improve the weather resistance of their infant incubators."

Mark groaned. If the electricity was already cutting out in October, there was no way the orphanage would survive when the real rainy season hit. Plus, knowing the African nation's crumbling infrastructure, chances were they wouldn't even get their lights on for weeks without outside help.

He was already booked to fly to Lebanon at the end of the month, and Nick was scheduled to be in Romania in December. Donations weren't as strong as they used to be, and the cost of airfare had skyrocketed.

"Shall I tell them we're grounded?" Nick offered.

"No." Since founding the charity three years ago, he had yet to turn down a single plea for help. He was not about to start today. "I've got two boxes of vinyl records back at the apartment. Rob from church has been eyeing them for months. Tell him we need the money for a trip. He'll make a generous offer."

"Will do." Relief flooded Nick's voice. "You know, I'm still not clear on who you're meeting tomorrow or what you're hoping to sell him."

Because you don't need to worry about it. "Just the deed to a small, useless piece of land."

"Huh. How are you feeling about it?"

So anxious he was almost sick to his stomach with stress. "Don't worry about it. I'm fine." At least that's what he was going to keep telling himself. Too many lives were counting on him for it to be any other way.

TWO

"Believe me, Officer," Ethan's voice crackled through the speakerphone. "I have absolutely no idea why one of my reporters would be in Cobalt."

The gray-haired officer sitting across from Katie raised his eyebrows. His shock mirrored hers.

No, I'm not crazy, she wanted to say. *My boss is just kind of incompetent. He's probably been drinking, and now he's forgotten. I even called him from the train.* She pressed her lips together. It had taken the police almost a half hour to get in touch with him as it was.

"You sent me up north to cover Jonah Shields's weekend gala," she said. "He's a real-estate developer. Remember?"

"In Kapuskasing," Ethan snapped. "Not Cobalt. Come on, Katie. You should have checked in there hours ago instead of running around rural Ontario getting yourself into trouble."

She pressed her fingernails into the palms of her hands, not knowing whether to scream or laugh.

The town of Kapuskasing was another five hours north. Even if her train hadn't been cut short she still wouldn't have made it there yet. Besides, what was he implying? That the terrifying ordeal she'd just gone through was somehow her fault?

She took in a long, deep breath and let it out slowly. *Focus, Katie. Just a few more weeks and you'll have the chance to prove why you should be editor. Impact News* was one of the smallest of the over three dozen publications put out by Comet Media. Ethan's aunt had a position on the board, which was how he'd gotten the job of editor four years ago. Not to mention how he'd managed to stay there despite the fact he spent far more of his time partying in the seedier nightclubs of downtown Toronto than he ever did actually doing his job. But last January, the board had seemingly gotten tired of watching as *Impact News*'s sales swirl down the drain from Ethan's reckless mismanagement, so they had given him until the end of the calendar year to pull his act together or find himself a new job. His day of reckoning was now less than three months away. When it arrived, Katie was going to be ready to go before the board with a proposal of her own.

"—I expect you to rectify this situation immediately," Ethan said. "Either you find a way to get to where you're supposed to be and cover this story as you've been assigned or you can consider yourself fired."

Of course, her carefully crafted plan relied on not getting fired between now and then. Which meant keeping Ethan happy, whether she liked it or not.

The older of the two officers—Sakes—was looking down at his notepad impassively. But the younger female officer—Parks—rolled her eyes up to the ceiling.

"Mr. Randall—" Officer Sakes cut him off "—the fact remains that someone attempted to kidnap Ms. Todd, and I can assure you that is something we are taking quite seriously—"

"And I'm telling you that my publication has nothing to do with it."

"No one is saying—"

"Random crimes happen all the time in small towns, I'm sure. Especially ones where the police presence is lacking."

Officer Sakes let out a long breath. Katie was used to Ethan's shouting. It was just a given that no matter what went wrong, his usual plan of attack was to defend himself loudly while others sorted it out. But here, in the safety of a police station, she was beginning to realize how irrational and out of control he must sound.

"Ethan." Her tone was gentle but firm. "It wasn't random. They knew my name."

There was a long pause on the other end of the

line. Then he swore. "Well, you're the journalist. I'm sure you can figure out a dozen ways some random thug could've seen your bank card or driver's license."

"Mr. Randall," Officer Sakes said, "is there anything else you can tell me about this assignment? Anything else that might be—" he grimaced "—helpful?"

Another pause.

"*Impact News* launched a new website not that long ago," Ethan said finally. "I believe our intern Chad posted something about Katie heading up to cover the Shields party…"

Of course. She should have thought of this before. Jonah Shields had made a lot of enemies. The real-estate developer had been a vulture when it came to preying on people who'd fallen on hard times. Just before Ethan had taken over as editor, she'd covered a failed attempt by the Langtry Glen Residents Association to stop Shields Corp from leveling an entire city block. The inner-city community had consisted of six low-income apartment buildings, a handful of family-run businesses and a drug rehabilitation drop-in program. Shields Corp had demolished it all to build luxury condos.

There was no end to the list of people who hated the Shields family. This weekend offered an unprecedented look inside their inner sanctum. What if someone had been after her press credentials to sneak into the event undetected and take their fight to Shields's home turf? The media was sure to have reported that the train wasn't running past Cobalt. What if it was just a crime of opportunity? They'd been looking for a reporter, and she happened to be alone?

"Thank you for your time, Mr. Randall," Officer Sakes said. "Someone will be in touch if we need anything else from you. Have a good night."

"Oh, no problem." Ethan seemed pleasant now. "And Katie, I'd like to see a story in by first thing tomorrow morning about how it felt to have your life threatened by evil scumbags. Never hurts to maximize every chance we get to drum up a few more readers—"

Officer Sakes didn't even bother trying to hide the look of disgust on his face. "Goodbye, Mr. Randall." Then he hung up the call.

Parks sighed loudly. She stood and gestured for Katie to join her in the hallway. "I'm going to go check in with the officers doing a sweep of Cobalt station to see if they've recovered your belongings. Shall I see about arranging overnight accommodations?"

Katie hadn't even thought that far yet. But of course she'd need a place to stay, and then tomorrow she'd somehow need to find a way to get to Kapuskasing. The damage on the tracks had been so extensive that trains weren't expected to start running again until Monday. This whole situation was out of control, not to mention grossly unfair. A hot flush of sudden tears rushed to her eyes. She blinked hard, forcing them to wait. "Thank you. Actually, just a phone book would be great. I'm sure I'll be able to find something."

"There's a courtesy phone in the waiting area. Feel free to take your time if there's anyone you want to call."

Right. "Is there somewhere I can freshen up?"

Parks nodded. "There's a ladies' room down the end of the hall."

It was all Katie could do to keep from bolting. But instead, she walked calmly, shoved through the door and then stood at the counter, gripping it hard with both hands. She forced deep breaths into her lungs. She was not going to let herself fall apart.

The water from the faucet was blissfully cold. She splashed it over her face. Then she ran wet hands through her hair and tied it back into a knot at the nape of her neck. She couldn't call her mother or her sister. They lived on the other side of the country. Besides, her stepfather and brother-in-law were the kind of harsh, controlling men she'd never consider being in debt to, even if they did feel inclined to let their browbeaten wives help her. Yes, she had a few friends at work but no one she'd ask to drive through the night to pick her up. As for church...

She swallowed hard. When she'd first moved to

the city for work six years ago, she'd started attending a wonderful, welcoming church on the Danforth. Tucked away in a cozy neighborhood, it was full of young professionals and new families. She'd even started attending a Bible study.

But when Ethan had taken over as boss at *Impact News,* four years ago, everything had changed. Long hours and stressful assignments had left her so tired it was tempting to just let herself sleep in on Sundays. When she first admitted to her church friends that—in exchange for a few more hours of unpaid overtime a week—she'd devised a plan to land herself the editorship, she'd been met with blank stares and the suggestion she rely instead on God to lead her into a new job.

Well, she'd tried that. For the entire first year she'd worked under Ethan, she'd prayed hard, sent out résumés and waited for God to show her a way out. But as the months dragged on without so much as an interview in sight, it became clear that simply waiting for rescue wasn't going to cut it.

The job market for journalists was shrinking, and too many papers were closing. She loved what she did too much to just give in and go back to waiting tables, like she'd done to pay her way through school. The only way to get ahead was to fight for her career. Fight for herself. Maybe God was still answering other people's prayers, but when it came to her own future, it sure felt like she was on her own.

"Ms. Todd?" Officer Sakes knocked on the door. "There's someone here to see you."

She pushed the door open, an unexpected warmth spreading out from her chest and down through her limbs as she saw Mark's tall, reassuring form. She'd never expected him to actually stay.

"How are you doing?" he asked. For a moment, the concern in his eyes almost made her want to cry again.

But when she spoke, her voice sounded stronger than she'd expected. "I'm okay. A little shaken up, obviously. But good."

He nodded like he understood more than she was actually saying. "I hope you don't mind, but there's someone here I'd like you to meet."

He stepped back. It was only then she saw the elderly black woman standing behind him. Long white braids cascaded down her generous frame. Laugh lines ringed her eyes.

"Katie, meet Celia. She runs a really wonderful and private guesthouse here in town. I've already taken the liberty of telling her about your situation, and she has a spare room tonight if you need a place to stay."

Conflicting feelings washed over Katie simultaneously, and all she could do was pinch her lips together and nod. Yes, she was grateful that Mark had gone to the trouble of finding her a place to stay. More grateful than she had words to say. But she was also unexpectedly resentful. She didn't need this strange man jumping to her rescue and offering to make arrangements on her behalf.

If watching her mother scrape and serve her self-centered father for years—only to welcome an even worse stepfather into their lives after his death—had taught her anything, it was that being dependent on the wrong man was far worse than going it alone. When Katie was sixteen, her older sister had given up a promising art career to marry a man just like them. That had been the final straw. That would not be her. She moved out two years later. Paid her own way through school. Bought her first car. Leased her first apartment. Worked hard to earn every byline in her portfolio. She'd made it this far on her own. So who was Mark to come along now and treat her like a lost little lamb?

"Ms. Todd?" Officer Parks walked down the hallway toward them. "I'm afraid I have some bad news. It looks like whoever tried to kidnap you took all your belongings with them. Is there anything in your bag that would lead them to the location that you're heading to next? The last thing we'd want is for them to get there first and lie in wait for you."

THREE

The words hit her like a blow to the chest. In that terrifying moment when Al had thrown open the back of his van and she'd seen the roll of duct tape lying on the floor, her only impulse had been to escape. But now, thanks to hurling her suitcase at Billy, she'd lost everything—including her laptop and camera. Not to mention the keys to her apartment. All she had left were her wallet, the clothes on her back and a cell phone that still couldn't get a signal.

Now she had potential stalkers to worry about?

"There was a printout of my hotel reservation in my bag," Katie said. "I guess I'm going to have to change where I'm staying now."

"That would be wise," Officer Parks said. "Was your home address on anything?"

She nodded. "I grabbed my mail on my way out, including some bills. But why would that matter? Is there any reason to think they'd come after me again?"

Parks pressed her lips together. "It is likely the men behind it have moved on to find another target. But still, we like to advise people to be cautious. We'll warn Toronto police to keep an eye on your apartment in case anyone shows up there and tries to get in with your keys. You'll want to change your locks. Of course, your suitcase may still turn up. We do still have people searching the area."

"I'd like to go back there and take a look myself, actually," Katie said. "There may be something I'll remember that could be helpful." She noticed Mark looked away as she said it. Did he not approve? Not that it mattered. She was hugely grateful he'd been there when she'd needed help. But now she was going to be just fine on her own.

"Was there a return train ticket in your bag?" the officer asked.

Katie nodded. "For Sunday."

"We suggest you change your travel plans. If someone is still after you, it's best to be as unpredictable as possible and break from any usual or expected patterns."

Be unpredictable? For a second, Katie was almost tempted to laugh. Everything that had happened since she'd stepped off the train had felt so far out of her control that she was lucky she hadn't collapsed on the floor in a puddle of tears. She blinked hard.

No, she was not going to cry. She could manage this. She was going to manage this.

Celia stepped forward and pulled Katie into a warm, protective hug. For a moment, Katie was so surprised by the gesture that she just stood there, letting the older woman's long braids fall around her shoulders like a cape. She couldn't remember the last time someone had hugged her like that—generously, spontaneously, asking nothing in return. Celia stepped back. "Don't you worry. The good Lord must've known you were coming to my house tonight, because I just collected a round of things for the clothing bank this afternoon. I'm sure there'll be plenty there that fits you."

"Thank you." Katie glanced from Celia to Mark. "Thank you so much, both of you."

Mark looked deep into her eyes. "You will be safe there. I promise you that."

A shiver ran down her spine as a deeper, more vulnerable fear stirred inside her. It was one thing to accept her life was in danger from an unknown threat. It was another thing entirely to realize this strong, rugged and oh-so-good-looking stranger was willing to personally guarantee her safety.

Gravel crunched under Mark's feet. He shot a sideways glance at the beautiful woman walking stoically beside him. Their flashlights sent beams of light swinging back and forth along the train tracks. Pale waves of hair fell over Katie's face. Her eyes were inscrutable in the darkness. Celia had already gone back to the guesthouse to get a room ready, but Katie insisted on accompanying him and Sakes back to where he'd left his truck and transmitter so that she could take a look around the train station for herself. He could respect that. If his equipment had been stolen, he'd have been the same way.

The ground sloped steeply downhill. Katie stumbled. Instinctively, his hand reached for her elbow, offering his strength to steady her.

She brushed it off. "Thank you. But I'm okay."

The words were polite enough, but there was an edge to her tone that told him Katie was the kind of woman who'd rather stumble a bit than lean on someone else for support. He'd heard it in her voice when he told her that he'd called Celia on her behalf. It was a tone he knew all too well from his development work. One that said, *"Thank you, but I can take it from here."* He tended to see it as a sign that the project he was working on was finished and he could move on with a clear conscience. Okay then. As soon as he knew she was taken care of, he'd say his goodbyes and move on. He was good at that. Too many charity workers hung on to a project long after it was done. Not him. He'd never had a problem walking away. The police and Katie waited beside the tracks while he climbed down and retrieved the portable broadcast unit. The prototype was a complete broadcast studio, hidden inside a nondescript hard-backed case. In the right hands, a tool like that could change the world. If TRUST ever got the resources together to get the project off the ground.

They spent over an hour helping the police search around the station for Katie's bag. Sakes called the search off around midnight and sent everyone home for the night. Mark offered her a ride to Celia's in his truck, but she opted to ride with Sakes instead, saying she had a few last questions for the officer. Something told him that the reporter would be grilling Sakes about police procedures on attempted kidnappings all the way back to the guesthouse. Would having more facts make her feel any safer? Mark hoped so for her sake.

He watched as she twisted her sweat-soaked hair up into a knot at the back of her head and then let it fall again. They hadn't exchanged more than a couple of words since leaving the station. Instead, her face had been as set and guarded as a mask, leaving him to guess what might be going on underneath.

She climbed into the front seat of the police cruiser, and Sakes closed the door for her. Only then did Mark slide onto the cracked leather seats of his ancient pickup truck and pop the key in the ignition, praying it would start. The rusted red pickup had been ten years old when he'd bought it. Now it was practically prehistoric—with nothing but a zigzag maze of duct tape keeping the seat springs at bay. But it was all his. The first thing he'd bought with his first independently earned paycheck, and he loved it for that.

The engine roared to life. His satellite phone started ringing, with the African drumbeat he'd preset for his second in command. He turned off the truck. A call from Nick this late at night meant trouble. "Hey, what's up?"

Nick tried to chuckle. It was the noise he always made when he was trying to put on a brave face about something. Now it sounded more like someone was strangling him. "Mark? We've got a major problem."

Mark fought the urge to groan. No, they could not have a major problem—they simply did not have the capacity to handle one more problem. The bank account only had enough to cover the rent on their workshop for three more months. Ever since he'd founded the charity, they'd been running pretty close to the edge. Now they were just a hairbreadth from tumbling over.

"Jenny's beginning to have second thoughts about marrying me…."

Mark swallowed hard. He couldn't imagine how much pain Nick was in right now. He was crazy about her.

"She wants us to postpone the wedding for a year and get premarital counseling. It's this job. She says she's begun to dread every time she sees my name on call display because I'm about to tell her I'm hopping onto another plane, heading off for weeks to some dangerous, developing world war zone..." Well, considering how much travel their work entailed, she definitely had a point. "She still loves me. I know she does. She's just worried that the job is going to keep us from being able to build a life together..." His voice trailed off.

Mark blew out of a long breath. "Okay. Here's what we're going to do. You tell Jenny that you're canceling all trips for the next six months to give you time to work things through. Longer if she needs it. I'll tackle Romania and Lebanon both."

"Are you sure?"

"Of course I'm sure." *Just don't quit. Because I can't handle TRUST alone.* "Change my Lebanon flight to Monday." Taking time off to go camping with Zack would just have to wait. "I'll wrap Lebanon up in three weeks, then fly to Zimbabwe for a couple of months and then head on to Romania in January. Once the tickets are booked, email around to everyone and let them know the new schedule." He could hear Nick taking notes.

"But the tickets are nontransferable."

Right. They were booking economy flights these days—without a dime to spare for extras. "That's okay. When the banks open in the morning, get my grandfather's watch out of the safety deposit box and take it down to Packard Jewelry on Queen West. They'll give you enough to cover the flight changes.

Plus, if I'm traveling for six months, I can break the lease on my apartment and throw my stuff in storage. Why pay for a place no one's going to be living in?"

Six months' rent in exchange for helping three different charities change countless lives? It was a no-brainer.

Nick sighed. "And you're sure you're okay with that?"

Mark watched as Officer Sakes's taillights disappeared in the distance. "Absolutely. I've got nothing to stick around here for."

Celia lived in a small hundred-year-old farmhouse off a winding dirt road.

Sakes's cruiser was pulling out as Mark arrived. Mark waved. Katie stood on the front porch, staring up at the clouds with her arms crossed over her chest. But as soon as he cut the engine and climbed out, she smiled and walked over.

"All sorted?" he asked.

"Pretty much. Celia's found me enough clothes to last a year. Plus someone from her church brought over a suitcase. She even managed to borrow a laptop."

He wasn't surprised. "Celia's a force of nature. She used to work in the child rescue division of social services. Her husband passed two years ago, and they never had children of their own. She's probably been itching to have someone around to take care of."

She nodded. Then her smile faded slowly. "It's all really wonderful and kind of her. But…" Her gaze drifted toward the tree line. She sighed and frowned. "I'm not sure I'm comfortable with people making this kind of fuss about me."

He was sure that wasn't the easiest thing for her to admit to someone. She looked up at him, letting her hard, determined mask slip from her eyes for a moment, exposing the look of pure exhaustion behind. He wanted to slide his arms around her shoulder, let her head fall against his chest and let his strength envelop her. Instead, he slid his hands into his pockets. "I get it. I'm actually the same way. Somehow it always feels a whole lot easier for me to be the one going into a refugee camp or disaster zone to help someone else than it is for me to even let a stranger hand me a quarter when I'm short at the gas station."

Huh, he didn't think he'd ever really admitted *that* to someone before, either.

"I hear you."

An unfamiliar feeling fluttered in his chest. Those weren't just empty words to her—he thought—she meant them. It was as if, inside the outer beauty that she carried off so effortlessly, he'd caught a glimpse of someone actually capable of listening. Someone he might even be able to risk telling the truth about himself.

He looked away. He couldn't afford to think this way. Not now. People were counting on him. His company was on the verge of financial collapse. He was leaving the country in four days. Plus, he still hadn't figured out how he was going to face his father again. Even if he had been willing to let himself pause, pull up a chair and find out more about this brave, beautiful stranger who had just landed in his world—right now was not the time. "Have you figured out how you're getting back to Toronto tomorrow?"

"Actually, I'm planning on heading north. I'll be staying in Kapuskasing."

Then again, maybe he didn't have to leave her quite as soon as he'd thought. His father lived out in the country, only about twenty minutes north of Kapuskasing. "I'll be driving past that way myself tomorrow. I'd be happy to give you a ride."

He could almost see the tension melting from her shoulders.

"That would be wonderful. This whole assignment has been a total disaster from the beginning."

"Kapuskasing is pretty small. What kind of story are you up here covering?"

"A completely inconsequential one." She rolled her eyes. "Someone is holding a gala this weekend and, for some reason, my boss thinks parties are news."

Well, that answered the question of whether her

story was related to anyone he knew. While he'd met a handful of people in the town, none of them were the type to throw a gala, let alone the kind you'd invite the press to. "Do you want to talk about it?"

"Not really." She sighed. "I actually used to love my job, back when I wrote about things that mattered. Now I feel more like I'm trapped in it and have to fight my way out."

"I know that feeling, too." Whatever kind of reception he was going to receive from his father, it sure wouldn't be a party. His father's face flashed across Mark's mind. He remembered the callous curl of his lip when he was angry and then the relief that had coursed through Mark like rain when he'd finally found the courage to walk away. He'd lost track of the number of times his father had called TRUST asking to speak to his son. Mark had ignored the calls for years.

But now? Here he was reduced to handing over the last thing that remained of his inheritance. The small plot of land his grandmother had left him was set inside the family's lands. The will had stipulated he had to offer first rights of sale to his father. He just prayed his dad would give him a fair price for it. Not for his own sake but for the sake of all the charity projects that depended on him.

The farmhouse door swung open. Celia stepped out onto the porch.

Katie yawned. "Well, I guess I'd better go crash.

I've got a long day ahead of me tomorrow. See you tomorrow. Thank you for everything."

He smiled. "My pleasure."

Her hand brushed lightly against his arm. Then he watched as she walked back into the house. The door closed, and he stared at it a full minute, willing her to come back outside.

An unsettling feeling burrowed into the center of his chest. Unfinished. This whole thing with Katie felt unfinished, like a half-built circuit board sitting on his workbench. Like an engineering project he'd just started working on and would be forced to walk away from tomorrow. There was a story there, a puzzle he had only started to figure out. Why would someone try to hurt her? Would they try again? The idea that she was going to disappear from his life in a few hours was almost unfathomable.

Rule number one of running a charity like TRUST was never start something you couldn't finish. With so few hours left until she walked out of his life, he'd be lucky to even scratch the surface.

Katie followed Celia through a disorienting maze of rooms. Ornate tables bursting with flowers and knickknacks filled every spare corner to overflowing. Celia led her through the living room, opened what at first glance appeared to be a closet and showed Katie into a small bedroom, dominated by a four-poster bed. There was a huge bag of clothes on the bed and an old clunky laptop humming on the bedside table.

"Remember to take whatever you'd like," Celia said. "Don't worry about getting any of them back to me, either. Just donate to one of the clothing banks in Toronto when you can. The Lord knows they need it more than we do. Now, I'll go find you something from the kitchen."

She swept out again before Katie could say another word. By the time she'd changed into a pair of simple black leggings and an oversized shirt, Celia was back again, carrying a tray with bread, honey and jam. She pressed a mug of tea into Katie's hands.

"Now if you're still hungry, we've got plenty more food in the kitchen." Celia turned toward the door then stopped. "Don't worry. The Lord knows where you are and will make sure you get where you need to be." She closed the door behind her.

Faint rain tapped against the window. Trees shook in the breeze, scattering red and gold leaves against the glass. Somewhere out there in the darkness were two strangers who'd tried to kidnap her. Had they tossed her belongings in a ditch and moved on to find another victim? Or were they now poring through her things, plotting how and when they were going to get their hands on her again? Katie set down the tea and pulled a quilt around her like a shroud.

She couldn't remember the last time someone had made her a cup of tea, let alone told her not to worry. For that matter, she could barely remember what it felt like to just sit still and stare out a window. When she first started out as a journalist she'd been drawn to the hard work, the fast pace, the unrelenting schedule. In college, she'd volunteered for a community newspaper during the day and waited tables at night. Her first boss at *Impact News,* an aging newshound named Ron, had pulled twelve-hour days and expected the rest of his team to do the same. She'd never minded falling into bed exhausted at the end of the day because she'd always known she was doing something that mattered.

Then Ethan came along. Needy. Unpredictable. One moment he was excitedly happy. The next he was inexplicably furious—changing writers' assignments and entire layouts on a whim. He was in his late thirties with a boyish charm and manipulative need to get his own way that made him appear years younger. He'd apparently tried his hand at a tabloid in Los Angeles before crashing, burning and returning home to beg his aunt for a bailout. Several of the staff suspected he was addicted to prescription drugs. Most days he came in with the smell of alcohol on his breath.

If there was one consistent thing about Ethan, it was the kind of publication he wanted *Impact News* to become—a supermarket tabloid. Parties, weddings, affairs, divorces, gossip and rumors. Pictures of pretty people wearing expensive clothes and acting ridiculous. Jonah Shields's weekend gala was hardly the most frivolous story he'd assigned her—at least Shields was a powerful and influential recluse.

Her cell phone still couldn't find a signal. She tried the laptop. Someone at *Impact* had already posted an article on their website about her attempted abduction. Very few facts and a whole lot of rhetoric. Just how Ethan liked it. Then she clicked on the link underneath: *Impact News Invited to Jonah Shields's Gala Weekend.*

Being invited to a party was news now? Well, probably in Ethan's world. Although they'd received an invitation to the event—from Shields's personal secretary, Tim Albright—chances were dozens of other reporters had, as well. It was the first time the Shieldses had allowed reporters inside their secluded Ontario estate.

Did the Shieldses even know that she'd covered the residents' protests in Langtry Glen? Certainly, they'd never responded to her request for an interview. Although that kind of socially conscious reporting was miles away from what Ethan would be expecting now.

Still, the mere fact she was going up to cover the weekend's events had already gotten over two-hundred comments from readers—many of them full of anger directed at the Shields Corp.

The Shields family deserves to suffer for all the innocent people they put out of business.

Oh, great! They throw a swanky, "private" weekend of events all the way up north. How about coming down to Toronto and facing some of the real people you've hurt?

What happened to you, Ms. Todd? You think we don't remember when you were walking around Langtry Glen, pretending you cared that we were about to be thrown out on the street. Way to betray your principles.

Little did they know. She plugged "Jonah Shields" and "Shields Corporation" into her search engine and started digging. If he was inviting reporters into his home, there had to be a reason. Despite the company's very public name, the family itself had managed to keep itself well out of the media's glare. Jonah Shields, a self-made man, had started gutting, developing and reselling homes straight out of high school. By the time he was twenty-five, he was running his own construction company. One of his first purchases was a resort hotel complex he'd bought for next to nothing from an owner facing foreclosure, which he'd then converted into his home and business headquarters. That's where she'd be heading tomorrow.

Jonah's wife had died when the children were young. Drug overdose. He had two grown children—a son, Jonah Junior, who had inexplicably left no internet trail, and a daughter named Sunny, who had taken over running much of the family business.

Two years ago, Shields had abruptly dropped from public view. All new building projects were put on hold—including Langtry Glen. Pundits wondered if he was sick. Critics theorized he was just preparing for something big. Now the tyrant was throwing a party.

Katie woke up with a jolt and stared out into the blackness. The laptop lay dead on the bed from where she'd fallen asleep reading. She stretched slowly as everything that had happened came rushing back into her mind in a cacophony of disjointed images.

The leer on Al's face. The empty van with a roll of duct tape lying on the floor. Fear pounding in her heart as she ran for the railroad tracks. Billy knocking her down and dragging her back. Mark pulling her into his arms. Feeling safe there.

She felt for the light switch and flicked it up. Nothing. A bolt of fear shot up her spine. Why was the power out? Had her kidnappers found her and for some reason cut the power? She took a deep breath and forced her heart to settle. No, she was going to be rational about this. Chances were the bulb had just blown and everyone was asleep. The most logical thing to do was to just go back to sleep and wait until the sun came up in the morning.

Katie closed her eyes again, but almost immediately, Al's face swam into her mind. She climbed out of bed. At the very least, it would help her sleep better if she went into the kitchen and made herself a cup of tea. She picked up the tea tray, slid the door back and stepped into the darkness.

A hand clamped around her ankle.

FOUR

She kicked out hard at the figure crouched on the floor, nearly losing her balance and falling through the open bedroom door. Dishes tumbled off the tray, onto the carpet. He let go of her ankle and leaped to his feet. She swung. The tea tray caught him hard against the side of the head. He stumbled back.

Dropping the tray, she sprang toward the gap of light filtering through the living room doorway. But before she'd taken a step, she felt a hand land on her shoulder.

"Katie—" A deep voice growled her name.

She swung her elbow back, landing it hard in his stomach. His grip tightened. Her mouth opened to scream but was instantly stifled by a strong hand clamping over her mouth. He spun her around, pinning her between the door frame and the warmth of his chest.

"Katie. Stop." His voice came hard and fast in her ear. "It's okay. You're safe."

Safe? But as much as her brain wanted to believe

that, the adrenaline coursing through her body was hardly about to allow that. She raised her hand to strike him again, but his hand slid off her shoulder and down onto her wrist. "It's me. Mark." He ran the back of her fingers along the side of his face as if to prove it to her. Her body relaxed. He eased his fingers away from her mouth.

"Mark?"

"Yeah. Trust me. You're okay."

She gently pulled her hand from his grasp. Her fingertips brushed the rough lines of his jaw. Then her hand slid onto his chest until she could feel his heart beat hard against her palm. His ragged breath brushed against her face. She shivered. He pulled her body closer into his chest, and for a moment— just one moment—she let him hold her there.

It had been a very long time since Mark had felt a woman touch him that way.

Tender. Trusting.

"I'm sorry. I didn't mean to scare you, Katie." He could feel her name slipping out over his lips like a whisper. He reached out and brushed his fingers against the back of her hand. The warmth of her smooth skin tugged at feelings he'd tried so hard to push to the corners of his mind.

Get a grip. She was frightened and looking to him for support, nothing more. Besides, trekking from one disaster zone to another wasn't exactly the kind of life you could bring a wife into.

She pulled away. He stood back, and he let her go.

"What were you doing on the floor?"

He rolled the answer around in his mind for a moment and then settled for total honestly. "I was sleeping on the couch. But it wasn't long enough to stretch out. So I ended up lying on the floor." Outside her door. Somehow he'd felt safer that way—knowing that nothing could get to her without going through him first.

He'd never expected she'd put up such a fight. For a moment, he'd actually thought she was going to get away and scream the house down until Celia woke up and called the police. Then again, maybe he shouldn't have been surprised. Her hand brushed against his. He stretched out his fingers in case she wanted to take his hand again.

She didn't. "I tried to turn the lights on, but nothing happened."

He felt for a lamp and flicked the light switch. Nothing happened. "Probably just a blown fuse. Believe me, it happens all the time in this place. Nothing to worry about. I'm sure there are candles in the kitchen."

She followed him across the living room, through the hallway and then into the dining room. A small trickle of light was seeping through the wide glass doors. Then she walked past him, making a beeline for the hutch. "We've got candles and even matches."

Blinking in the gloom, he stared at the complicated metal sphere as she carried it over and set it down on the dining room table. She lit a match, cradled the flame in her palm, then leaned over and lit a tiny white candle buried somewhere deep inside the structure. Then a second and a third. There must have been at least two dozen tea lights balanced precariously on the thing.

Who on earth designed these things? What was the point of a lighting fixture where the first light was destined to burn out by the time you made it all the way around to lighting the last one?

If only he hadn't left his own flashlight in the truck.

He yanked open a drawer and started rooting around for a flashlight.

Her hand gently flitted from one candle to another. "This is beautiful." Little glowing flames flickered in her eyes. "I had been thinking of looking for a flashlight, but when you mentioned candles…"

He slammed the drawer shut again and rubbed his hand over his hair. Had he really mentioned candles? He was certain he'd been thinking about flashlights. At least he hoped he'd been. But somehow being around her kept making the wires between his brain and his mouth short-circuit. He sat down across from her and looked out the sliding glass doors into the blackness beyond.

Silence spread out between them, punctuated only by the sound of light rain rustling in the trees outside. Katie's fingers brushed over the edges of the candles, spinning them gently to one side and then the other. "A couple of months ago, this writer from a rival publication was abducted and attacked by her ex-boyfriend. She fought him off and escaped." She bit her lip slowly. "It was all over the news. Ethan stuck her picture up on the wall and berated us all for not being more like her...whatever he thought that meant. But, to be honest, some of us were almost jealous of her. You know...for being a hero. Surviving. I'm realizing now I should've been praying for her."

She shrugged, and her slim shoulders looked lost in a flowing shirt at least three sizes too big. Somewhere, deep inside his chest, Mark could feel himself wanting to just gather her into his arms.

"I know I escaped, but..."

"But you still don't feel totally safe?"

One of the candles flickered and died. She scanned his face—like he was a piece of equipment sitting on the workbench.

He cleared his throat. "In case I haven't said it, I am really sorry about what happened tonight." He might not be able to take away the memory of what had happened, but he could at least try to soften it a little by letting her know she wasn't alone. "I've been there. I know it's not exactly the same thing, but my partner, Nick, and I were threatened at knifepoint by a taxi driver in Somalia last year." Had Nick told Jenny? Probably. Another reason why she'd have second thoughts about the wedding. "The guy drove us around for a bit, took all of our stuff and then eventually let us go. But it was pretty scary there for a while. Then afterward…I had all these crazy thoughts running through my mind. What if I had picked a different taxi? What if I'd been wearing something different? Or acted differently? What if…" His voice trailed off, and she nodded.

"It's one of the risks you run traveling to the kind of places I do," he added. "Once in Nairobi, people actually broke into our hotel room and ransacked it while we pretended to be asleep."

"You didn't try to stop them?"

"They had guns, and our stuff wasn't worth all that much. I wasn't going to risk my life and theirs by fighting them for something I could replace. I'll risk my life for another life but not for my wallet or suitcase. You remember what I said about novices and guns? They get cocky but don't have the necessary skills to handle a weapon safely, let alone hit what they're aiming at. Especially if they're big ones, like an AK-47. Although, for the record, AKs always pull up and to the right, by the way, so if someone waves one in your face drop down and to the left."

A tiny laugh escaped from the corner of her lips, sending shadows dancing down the lines of her neck.

"Seriously though," he added, "it can get pretty hairy out there at times, so we've developed a few little tricks and things to help minimize the risk. Like a moisturizer that has the added benefit of loosening adhesives like duct tape. It's made of eucalyptus oil. I use it all the time actually because eucalyptus is also a natural insect repellant. We even added a sunscreen to it."

A soft light was twinkling in her eyes again. He felt his heart lift.

"How did you get into this kind of work?"

Mark opened his mouth. Then he shut it again. He'd never been asked that question before. "I was actually taking engineering in college," he said, "when one Sunday in church, one of the guys who works for me now—Nick Abrams—got up and gave this talk about a missions trip he was going on to help install toilets for a charity in Belize. He was in college, studying to be an electrician. I was looking at the pictures up on the screen and realized there were some simple things they could do to really improve on the design. So I went up to him afterward, and he put me in touch with the charity."

A second candle flickered and died. He reached

across the table for the matchbox. It was empty. "We ended up going together. I had a knack for designing. He was great at building things. We went on three more trips together that year. Six the second. Eighteen the third. We started calling ourselves TRUST. Until one day we looked at each other, and asked, why not do this full-time?"

He took a deep breath and looked down at his hands. He'd never actually told anyone this. "That really upset my father. He wanted me to come work for him, and he's not the kind of man who's good at taking no for an answer, especially from his son. But then my grandmother died and left me a little bit of money. Enough to offer Nick a small salary and give TRUST a head start. I wanted to tell Dad in person. Man to man. He started yelling. Called me foolish. Told me I was ruining my life and that he was ashamed of fathering a son who'd do something so financially irresponsible. I said I was ashamed to be the son of a man who cared about nothing but money." He ran his hand over the back of his neck. "We both said some pretty horrible things. I knew I needed to apologize. I just told myself it was best to wait until everyone had calmed down. Somehow I never got around to calling. That was three years ago."

Silence filled the space between them again, and somehow he was thankful for it. He was almost relieved she hadn't jumped in with platitudes or said something stupid like, "But he's your father!" or "Don't you miss him?"

Of course he was and of course he did. It still felt like a punch in the gut every time he saw his father's name on his phone. But loving someone wasn't always the same as knowing how to get along with them.

Her fingers brushed across his. Just for a moment. He looked up. Her eyes hadn't left his face. "And you invent things?" Her tone was gentle. Like someone who was used to asking questions and knowing when someone wanted to change the subject. He was grateful.

"I do. Although mostly I improve on things other people have designed, figuring out how to make them more cost effectively and efficiently. Lately, I've been working on a portable radio broadcast studio and transmitter. It's intended to help get emergency information out after major disasters any time the traditional modes of communication are down. Could be a real game changer in global disaster response."

To his surprise, she frowned. "I miss having what you have."

"What?"

She picked up the matchbox and rolled it around in her fingers. "Well, you love your job, don't you? I used to love mine, too. When I first got the job at

Impact News it was amazing. I got to visit all sorts of cool places and write about how they were making a difference in the community. But then my current editor, Ethan, was hired, and all he cares about is making money." She sighed. "I hate some of the stories he assigns."

"Then why don't you quit?"

Something flashed across her eyes. Was it anger? No, it looked more like frustration. He'd obviously hit a nerve.

"I have bills to pay, and there aren't a lot of good jobs going around. It's not like I can afford to take a leap of faith and trust everything is going to be all right." She tossed her hair out around her shoulders. For a moment, Mark could feel the scent of her perfume rise in the air around him. His eyes traced down the folds of her sleeves as she crossed her arms across her chest. She wasn't so much slender as lithe—he realized—and strong, like a threatened animal on the edge of flight.

"Besides, I have a plan. In three months' time, Ethan's going to get dragged before the board of directors to explain why the newspaper has been performing so miserably. When they do, I'll be ready." She took in a deep breath and let it out slowly. "I haven't really told anybody this before. But ever since January, I've been secretly creating my own sample version of what the publication could be like."

"I'm not sure I understand."

Katie stood up and walked around behind her chair, grabbing the back with both hands. "You build prototypes, right? Well, have you ever had to make a prototype of something just to prove to someone that it was possible?"

He nodded. All the time. In fact, it could be highly frustrating to know he had a brilliant idea in his head but had to actually build it before anyone would believe him. If he could find the words to just describe for people what he could see inside his mind, he'd be far more productive.

Katie let go of the chair and leaned back against the sliding glass door. "When I discovered my editor was kind of on probation, I told my old boss that I was ready to march into the company boardroom and tell them that, as editor, I could create a far better paper. He said, 'Don't. Until you can prove it.' It's not like the board—which includes Ethan's aunt, by the way—was about to take my word for it. So, I started writing every article Ethan assigned me twice—the fluff way he wanted for the paper and my own hard-hitting, investigative version. He sends me to cover Free Donut Day in High Park, and I write a story about the city promoting refined sugar when we're facing a child obesity crisis. He tells me to write about his friend's new clothing line, and I uncover the garments were created with sweatshop labor."

He whistled. "And what are you doing with these stories?"

"Saving them until the time is right. My own private story arsenal to create my own prototype of the newspaper."

Wow. The dedication that must take was impressive. "Your boss doesn't know?"

She shook her head. "No, but a couple of colleagues do. I do the job I'm paid to do first and then write the others on evenings and weekends." Her shoulders rose and fell. "I don't take time off, really. I have about three years' worth of vacation days saved up at this point anyway. It's like working two full-time jobs."

He knew that feeling. TRUST was a round-the-clock lifestyle. He'd lost count of the number of times he'd sat down at his workbench, intending to finish just one more circuit before packing it in for the day, only to look up and see the morning sun creeping through the window. "But at least I know every prototype I make has the potential of changing someone's life," he said. "It's not like I'm creating them and just hiding them away in a drawer."

Her arms folded tightly across her chest. "I'm not hiding anything. I'm building a portfolio. My contract states I can't pitch to other publications, and

I'm not about to trust my stories to a self-absorbed junkie like Ethan." Another candle flickered and died. The ice in her voice was so sharp that he nearly flinched.

"I didn't mean it that way." His voice dropped to the soothing tone he found usually helped smooth over misunderstandings when he was on building sites. "I just happen to know something about what it's like to live with a workaholic." He'd intended to sound reassuring, like he was looking for common ground. But judging by the way her eyebrow arched, it had come across as anything but.

"I'm not a workaholic," she said. "I believe in what I do. I'm dedicated to it. And I'm just doing what it takes to survive in the real world."

He frowned. "That's what my father used to say. He practically never looked up from his desk my whole childhood. It destroyed his marriage and our family—"

"I'm really sorry. That must have been terrible. But I'm pretty realistic about knowing I don't have time for a relationship with anyone, let alone marriage or children. Not until my career is further off the ground."

Well, they had that much in common. Her tone of voice was that of a sympathetic professional now. As though she actually felt sad for the boy he'd been— the kid so desperate to earn his father's approval before he'd learned the hard way it wasn't coming.

But that gentle, unguarded warmth he'd heard there just a few moments ago had melted away. "I have three more months of this. Tops. This is just temporary."

Yeah, every workaholic he knew had said that. "But what if the board decides to let your boss keep his job?"

Her back arched against the window as though she was trying to back away from the thought. Suddenly, he found himself missing her smile.

"Then I guess I'll just have to work harder and come up with another plan. I'm not just going to give up."

"All right, but—"

"When was the last time you took a vacation, Mark?"

Touché. "I was supposed to go camping with a friend this week. But—" *But I'm hopping on a plane Monday.* "Something came up, and now I have to work. It's not the same thing though."

"Because you're out there changing lives, and I'm just a writer who covers ridiculous parties?"

Okay. That was *not* fair. That's not what he had meant. *Was it?* There was the clatter of a garbage can falling over on the deck outside. Celia probably had raccoons. He'd take a look at how she secured her bins tomorrow.

Katie's head hadn't turned. Then again, if she lived in the city she'd probably gotten used to tuning out background noise. But in the kind of places he traveled, a keen sense of hearing was sometimes the only thing stopping you from losing half your gear in the night.

"What I do matters, too." Katie's voice rose. "It used to, anyway. And one day it will again when I'm actually able to go back to writing hard-hitting, investigative pieces like covering how the loss of the Langtry Glen drug rehabilitation center devastated a community—"

Another crash outside. This was louder. Hang on. Were the shadows playing tricks on him, or was there actually someone out there?

He held up a hand. But she didn't seem to notice.

"—instead of having to cover the fact Jonah Shields, the big, bad developer responsible, is holding a party."

Mark jumped out of his seat, his mind momentarily paralyzed as two thoughts hit him at once like dueling claps of thunder. Katie was talking about his *father*.

And a hooded figure was outside the window with a camera.

FIVE

In a heartbeat, Katie's emotions went from mild frustration to white hot panic as she watched Mark leap to his feet. What was happening? What had he seen? Her head began to turn. But in an instant, the timbre of his voice made her freeze.

"Don't. Move."

His eyes met hers. Serious. Focused. With such a single-minded intensity that the dark forest-green iris of his eyes almost faded to black. Then a light-hearted smile spread across his face that looked so genuine she would have almost believed it was real. He stretched out his hand. "Come here. Let's go sit in the other room."

The cold sliding window pressed up against her neck. She willed her feet to move. They didn't. Panic dripped down her spine, paralyzing her limbs. She could hear movement behind her back now. Someone was there. Inches away from her. Separated only by a thin sheet of glass. Someone who had hunted her like an animal, and now had her in his sights.

Did he have a gun? Her eyes glanced over Mark's shoulder toward the hallway. Even if she ran, there's no way she'd be able to outrun a bullet and the spray of flying glass.

"Katie." The authority in his voice cut cleanly through her fear like a knife. Mark stepped toward her. "Trust me."

She stumbled forward and slid her hand into his. His fingers tightened around hers. Could he feel how badly she was trembling? He turned them toward the hallway. Everything in her wanted to run, but his arm slid around her shoulder, pulling her into his side, forcing them to walk.

"There's someone outside, isn't there?" she whispered into his neck.

He nodded.

"Does he have a weapon?"

"Not that I can see. But he was holding a camera."

A camera? But why would someone take their picture? Had he been watching her all night? Taking pictures through the bedroom window while she'd been sleeping?

"It's safer for everyone if we don't startle him until you're out of harm's way." Mark added, "He hasn't moved since I spotted him, so he may not have realized I saw him. Just go into Celia's room, lock the door and call the police."

She squeezed his hand slightly and rolled her shoulders back until he let her go. Then she strode calmly ahead of him into the hallway, knocked twice on Celia's door and then turned the handle and stepped inside. "What are you going to do?"

"I'm going to get that camera."

Mark turned back toward the dining room.

She risked a glance over her shoulder and caught a glimpse of Billy through the glass. The teenager turned and sprinted off into the night. Mark ran after him. She shut the door, braced her hands against the door frame and tried to slow her racing pulse. A flashlight switched on behind her. Celia sat up in bed looking tired but alert.

"Sorry to wake you." Katie crossed over to the bed. "Everything's okay…" Oddly, as she said those words she felt them to be true. "Mark saw someone outside. He suggested I wait with you and that we call the police."

And somehow she'd just trusted him…

She sat down on the bed and stared at the door. *Dear Lord, please keep him safe.* She couldn't remember the last time she'd really prayed for anything. But as she felt the words rushing through her heart, a gentle peace followed.

Celia had the phone in her hand. "The phone line is dead."

"How about a cell phone?"

"We don't have any reception around here."

For a moment, Katie felt the new and fragile peace about to slip from her grasp.

But then the older lady took her by the hands and bowed her head. "Oh, Lord. Like the psalm says, you have searched us and you know us. You perceive our thoughts from afar—"

There was a knock at the door. "Katie?"

She jumped up. "Yeah?"

"He's gone."

She opened the door. Mark looked so tired and worn that for a moment it took everything in her to keep from just slipping her arms around him and letting him lean against her for support.

"The phone's down."

"That's okay. We can call the police on my satellite phone."

Mark gripped his coffee mug with both hands and watched as the sun slipped over the horizon. The officers who had answered his call were different from the ones they'd spoken to last night, and the one taking Mark's statement made no attempt at hiding the fact he thought his time was being wasted.

According to Officer Smith, a downed tree had taken out both the power and phone lines. The young, square-jawed officer had then added that it was a common hazard of being in a rural area, as if Mark was some sheltered city dweller who'd never stepped outside his office before.

He gritted his teeth and focused on just getting through the officer's questions. This one arrogant man was not going to rob him of either his patience or self-control.

Yes, the man had been a slender build. Yes, he was certain it was the same young man who had tried to kidnap Katie from the station. Yes, he was certain that he had a camera in his hands. But the figure had already been halfway across the yard when Mark had opened the door, and he'd taken off running into the woods. Yes, he was absolutely positive it hadn't been a large raccoon or a bear.

An hour later, Mark was pacing circles around the truck. His mind was tossing up questions he couldn't even begin to find an answer for.

The officer had been especially skeptical about Mark's motives for chasing after Billy. So what if the boy had a camera? The harder Mark tried to explain that he'd been trying to protect Katie's honor from prying eyes, the more he'd come to realize he'd suddenly reacted out of an old, ingrained instinct born from years of watching his father's security guards chase away the paparazzi. As a boy, he'd wanted to protect his younger sister from the media's glare, when at his mother's funeral a crowd of cameras vied for pictures of her tears. No wonder their father had sequestered them inside the walls of the family complex in northern Ontario, insisted they don baseball caps and sunglasses in public and hidden them behind their car's tinted windows. That privacy, at least, was one thing he could thank his father for. When Mark had left home, there'd been very few childhood pictures of him floating around the internet. Then, he'd learned the technical skills to further erase what little there was of his digital footprint. While there were plenty of people who had reason to hate Shields Corp, very few were obsessed enough to study his family so thoroughly they'd have recognized his adult face.

But still, his name had haunted him.

Jonah Mark Shields Junior.

That was what his parents had chosen to name him when he was born—Junior. They hadn't even given him a real name to call his own. Sure most people had called him Mark—especially his sister. But every time he saw his name on a piece of paper it was a reminder that he wasn't even a full-fledged person in his family's eyes. Merely an extension of his father.

That was how the world had treated him, too. With a mixture of fear and contempt. Women had pretended to like him until they realized he didn't actually have a cent of his father's money. People had deferred to him, but he could never be sure who actually liked him.

He'd walked away, changed his name, cut himself off from his past. But still, it was always there, threatening to sneak up on him. That was one of the things he loved so much about being in small, third-world villages in far-flung parts of the world.

There he could be sure of being known as himself, and not just as an extension of his father.

The screen door creaked then clattered. Mark jumped. Katie was standing on the front porch. Vibrant blue-and-turquoise cloth cascaded from her waist down to her knees. Her slender frame was set off perfectly by a navy top and cream-colored jacket. Her long blond hair was tied back in a loose knot at the nape of her neck. Her face, clean of makeup, caught the sun as she moved. Mark's mouth went dry.

The memory of her fingers curling against his hand slipped into his mind. What must it have taken for someone that strong and determined to have been willing to place her life in his hands? To be trusted by someone like her was an honor, a responsibility. And what was he doing with it? Staring at her like some teenager mooning over his first crush? No, she deserved better than that. A woman like her deserved to be courted. To be taken out on a proper date to the kind of restaurant he wasn't about to be able to afford. Besides, he was leaving the country on Monday, for six months, maybe more. Then when he returned, between his work and hers, they'd just end up breaking each other's hearts like Nick and Jenny or his father with his mother.

While waiting for his turn to be questioned, he'd skimmed through some of Katie's newspaper articles online. Not just the newer fluffy ones but older ones she'd written before Ethan had become editor. What he read impressed him even more. She had a flair for words, but she also had heart. When he'd gotten to the piece about Langtry Glen, he'd had to put his machine away. He didn't want to know what she'd said about his father.

That's when it hit him. In all the years he'd known his father, he'd never once thrown a party or allowed media within the family complex. When Katie had mentioned she was heading up north to cover a gala, it had never even occurred to him that his privacy-seeking father was about to throw open his doors. So, why had he decided to throw a gala the very weekend Mark was traveling up to meet him? Let alone one he was inviting the media to?

The mere thought sent chills running up the back of his neck. He'd not been in touch with his father personally about meeting. He'd instead contacted his father's private secretary, Tim Albright, who had instructed him when to come.

Had the party been booked before or after Jonah had discovered his estranged son was coming home? Was this his father's way of punishing him? Nick kept telling him they needed to develop a media strategy to deal with the inevitable day that a reporter called to ask why a small, humanitarian charity was being run by Jonah Shields's son. Even though his father and sister had nothing to do with TRUST, if a scandal-seeking reporter started throwing around unfounded allegations about some underhanded link, it could be the charity's death knell.

As long as the company stayed small, grassroots and under the radar, the day someone might find a link between TRUST and Shields Corp had seemed too far off to worry about. Until now.

But one thing was certain. As long as Katie's life was in danger, he wasn't leaving her side. He'd get her to Kapuskasing safely. Then he'd decide what to do about his father.

Celia had followed Katie out onto the porch. As the two women hugged, he caught Katie glancing his way. His eyes met hers, and her eyebrows raised. Had she read the expression on his face?

The trees rustled gently behind him. The wind had better not be picking up again. Needing something to keep his hands busy, he pulled out the sleek silver case housing the broadcast unit prototype. He rested it on the back of the truck and snapped it open. His heart caught in pride as the compact yet powerful equipment inside purred to life.

As the faint sound of Katie's laughter drifted across the yard toward him, he found himself fighting the urge to go over and ask what was so funny. Celia slipped something into her hand. If Katie discovered who his father was, would she feel obligated to tell the people she worked with that she was driving up to Kapuskasing with Jonah Shields's own son? Judging by what he saw of the newspaper's website, it seemed exactly the kind of secret they'd be all over exposing in big capital letters. He could avoid the press who were descending on his father's home by rebooking the visit with his father. But he had promised Katie that he would drive her north and was not about to abandon her now. Would her employer try to force her to write about him in order to keep her job? There was no way he'd make her choose between keeping her job and protecting his identity.

Even worse, what if the news of who she was traveling with put her life in even further danger? As much as he hated the idea of having some irresponsible media outlet all over his business, the idea of somehow jeopardizing Katie's life made telling her about his past almost too risky to bear. No, he'd tell her when he got her there safely. Either that, or he'd drop her off, get on a plane and fly out of her life. If she found out the truth later, he'd just have to hope she'd understand why he kept it secret.

She walked across the lawn toward him. "Ready to go?"

"Pretty much. Did you manage to get through to your office?"

"I did. They're really going overboard with covering my trip online now."

"I saw." He tried not to roll his eyes. Then he smiled slightly to see that she was rolling hers.

"They'd have probably written an entire piece on

what I had for breakfast this morning if I'd told them," she said. "The paper is playing it like some kind of grand conspiracy now. Were Billy and Al trying to steal my identity so they could sneak some-one into the event? Will they try again? I can just imagine Ethan gleefully rubbing his hands together and hoping something even worse befalls me. I can't wait for this story to be over."

You and me both.

"Is that the transmitter unit? Can I see it?"

He spun it toward her. The sturdy case housed a thin tablet computer, two microphones, mixers and a state-of-the-art transmitter. "It's basically the world's smallest, all inclusive, portable radio studio." An un-expected thrill ran through his heart as he heard her gasp. "It has a pretty long battery life but can also run off a simple car battery. Think blackout, hur-ricane, terrorist attack—basically it's a way to get information out safely anytime traditional broadcast systems are down." He quickly walked her through the set up and tutorial. "You can broadcast live, just like any normal radio station. Plus we've even com-piled a directory of common emergency sounds and warnings that you can just activate and run." His hands flickered over the touch screen. "Let's pre-tend a tsunami just hit and you want to warn people about potential aftershock waves."

A series of sound waves popped up on the screen. He hit Play. Eight long beeps played, and then the screen went black. He tapped the keys in vain, but the whole machine had frozen. For a moment, he battled the urge to curse, pushing the words out of his mind before they reached his lips. Those words were part of the world he grew up in—the cruel, ruthless edge of his father's world—not the man he was now.

To her credit, Katie didn't laugh.

"I'm guessing this audio file is corrupted," he said.

"Thank God you caught it."

His eyes scanned her face. She seemed sincere. He smiled. "Yeah, thank God." He dug a tattered notebook from the recesses of his bag. A pen was hanging from the spine by a leather strap. When he pulled the pen out, the strap broke free. Figured. He snapped the strap off the pen and then made a note in his log. "Tsunami file corrupt." He sighed. It was item 127 on an ever expanding list of bugs and problems that needed fixing. Starting with the fact that if he didn't disable the transmitter before it booted up, the unit now had the disconcerting fault of trying to take over every frequency in the area.

Yet, with the right funding, the project had such incredible potential. So many of his inventions did. One night he'd been praying, down on his knees, begging God to help him see a way forward, when he found himself thinking about the small patch of land his grandmother had left him. It was an island, in fact—only a few thousand square feet—set inside a lake on the Shields property. Big enough for a family home, not much more. It was the only piece of the Shields complex his father didn't own.

Initially, Mark had gotten an almost selfish pleasure from knowing it was there, a burr in his father's side. A reminder that the almighty Jonah Shields didn't control everything. But down on his knees, beside his workbench, he'd sensed he needed to check his attitude. The resentment needed to go. He needed to swallow his pride and offer it back to his father, having faith that whatever he'd get for it would be enough to carry TRUST through whatever came next.

Once he'd set his mind to do it, the sense of spiritual peace that he'd felt had made everything seem clear. But now the whole situation seemed so murky it was hard to see how God could have ever been guiding it.

"What's that?" Katie's voice broke into his thoughts. He looked down and realized he'd twisted the strap through the fingers. A small but heavy silver medallion hung down into his palm. There was a shield in the center, crisscrossed by a sword and a cross. "My grandmother gave it to me when I was a teenager." He ran the tribal patterned braided leather through his fingers, thinking about why she had given it to him, what it had meant. "I threw it away almost immediately as part of my rebellious teenage phase and thought I'd lost it forever. But when she died, I discovered she'd somehow found it and saved it for me. She also left me a tiny plot of land, my grandfather's watch and the money I used to start TRUST. Oh, and her family Bible. She was the only one in my family who believed in God and the only one who believed in me." He dropped it into her palm. "Would you believe the pendant is actually a GPS tracker in disguise? My grandmother bought if for me when the technology first appeared on the market." Her eyes opened wide. "Oh, it's been disabled for years. Believe me, I scanned it first chance I got. Probably couldn't turn it on now if I wanted to."

He stretched out his hand toward her. She tied the band around his wrist, her fingertips brushing against the inside of his palm. He pulled his hand back, looked down at it thoughtfully. "I used to run away a lot, and as much as I wanted to just leave, escape and never return, there was also something comforting about knowing I could never be totally lost."

Katie leaned her head against the window as Mark eased the truck down the long unpaved road and then out onto the empty, rural highway. She was pleased to see the two police cars stationed at either side of the road, no doubt looking for the white van that had tried to abduct her the night before. She'd tucked her wallet into the outside pocket of the borrowed jacket and zipped her slim phone into the jacket's small inside pocket. The bag of clothes was stored with Mark's bags in the back of the truck.

"That eucalyptus cream I told you about is in the glove compartment, by the way," he said after a while. "In case you want to try it."

"Thanks."

"I'm telling you that you won't burn, and the bugs will stay away, too." He grinned. "It'll even help your skin retain its heat if you decide to take an impromptu swim. This is what I love most about what we do—finding those simple solutions."

There was a small white jar inside the glove compartment. He was right; it smelled wonderful. She tentatively rubbed some on her hands. Then she spread it down her arms before smoothing it onto her face. She put the jar away then glanced over at Mark again.

He seemed distracted, preoccupied. She read it in the lines on his forehead and the way his eyebrows would come together as if listening to an unsettling voice in the back of his mind.

Fair enough. She was feeling pretty unsettled, too. And not just because it seemed someone had first tried abducting her and then spied on her. Their middle of the night conversation in the dining room had really rattled her. She'd long given up on trying to build a relationship after finding far too many men simply didn't understand why she would turn down an evening out to write long into the night or give up her Saturday to cover a story. That didn't mean she was a workaholic. Just someone who loved what she did. But Mark's question of what she'd do if she couldn't rid herself of Ethan sat like a rock in the pit of her stomach.

Towering forest and harshly hewn rock spread out in front of them, blending into an endless expanse of gray and green, red and gold and with the occasional dash of blue. Her job had cost her what so far? Sunday morning church? Close friendships? The chance at a real romantic relationship? If Al and Billy really had been after her press credentials for the Shields event, her job might have even put her life in danger. What would it demand of her next?

"I'm sorry I dragged you into all this."

"I'm not." He smiled, the sun lighting up the green of his eyes. "In fact, I'm really thankful I was there."

"Me, too. I just hope I didn't mess up your plans."

Again, that look of concern crossed his face again. But all he said was, "Don't worry about it. What time is your event?"

"Four. But that's just a media meet and greet. The real thing starts tomorrow. There's a media brunch in the morning, then some free time we can use to tour the grounds and finally a huge gala at night. Thankfully, Celia was able to find a dress that will pass as a gown. You can just drop me off at the hotel whenever we get there, and they will send a car for me." She watched as his mouth opened and then quickly shut it again. "What's wrong?"

"I'm just working through some stuff, and I'm not really ready to talk about it with anyone."

"Okay." She reached over and squeezed his shoulder. "Well, I'm happy to listen if you change your mind."

A wide grin spread across his face. He really did have a wonderful mouth. Wide and expressive, like it was an overflow from the joy he was feeling inside. "Can I ask what was on the piece of paper Celia gave you?"

"Sure." She dug into her pocket. "In fact, you might appreciate it. It's a copy of Psalm 139. I'd told her that I was feeling lost in life, in general, and she gave it to me as a reminder that God always knows where I am."

"I always remember that one on rough plane flights," he said. "I like the bit about, 'If I rise to the heavens you are there. If I make my bed in the depths you are there.'"

She laughed. "Celia prayed it last night when you ran outside to confront that stalker. She wanted me to remember that no matter where we are and no matter what happens that God always knows where I am." Now, if only she could actually get herself to believe that. She glanced at the medallion on his wristband. "How much traveling do you do?"

"Tons. It feels like we're always on the run somewhere."

Katie leaned her head back against the seat. Yeah, she knew what that felt like. But her life was more like a treadmill. Always running. Getting absolutely nowhere. "Must be amazing to build your own company."

"I'm not so much building a business these days as trying madly to keep one from falling apart. Things have been rough. Donations are down. The cost of travel is up. We're being pinched from all sides. Some days it almost feels like we're just moments away from disaster."

Yeah, she knew that one, too. Silence spread out between them again, but it was a comfortable one. The landscape was lush but desolate. The road cut through towering slabs of rock. A never-ending stream of trees flew past the window, broken only by the rare glimpse of a lake or unpaved road.

She read through the words of the psalm to herself, her heart catching on the words, "All the days ordained for me were written in your book."

Had the Lord really planned her life? If so, then why had God allowed Ethan to take over the publication she loved so much? Why allow the job she loved to disappear? Why hadn't God stepped in, gotten her another job? She glanced over at the striking form of the strong man beside her. True, her current circumstances could be worse. Far worse.

As if reading her mind, Mark glanced toward her. "Are you sure you really want to cover this story? If you want to change your mind, I'm willing to drive you back to Toronto." He'd said it cautiously as though he was approaching a land mine that was about to explode under his feet.

"It's my job." She winced. Why had she sounded so defensive?

"Okay, I get that. But if it's making you unhappy or is putting your life at risk—"

"Doesn't your job ever put your life at risk?"

He bristled. "That's not the same thing."

Right. It was all right for his job to be demanding and dangerous but not hers. "Look, when I was training to be a journalist I took a few overseas trips with a charity to see what kind of work they were doing. I visited refugee camps and saw the effect of countries at war with themselves. You're not the only one who's ever taken risks—"

"I didn't say I was." Okay, so he sounded frustrated now. "I know you're plenty strong and brave. But this is different—"

"Why? Because Shields is using zoning laws and banking rules to ruin people's lives instead of weapons? Have you heard of Langtry Glen? It was the last solid news story I covered before Ethan became the boss."

He sighed deeply. "I have. But I don't know much about it."

"Did you know the buildings were all city-owned, subsidized properties run by Toronto Community Housing?" He shook his head. She kept going. "They set aside properties especially for people living below the poverty line either because they can't find steady work or are on some kind of assistance. There were six apartment blocks, a few small businesses and a drop-in center for people trying to get off drugs and alcohol. It was this little oasis in the city for people who had fallen on hard times and needed a hand up.

"But then it started to have a drug problem. Rumor was a drug dealer had moved into the building and started supplying drugs to some of the more vulnerable, low-income residents—not to mention catching people coming to the drug program and tempting them to relapse.

"So the residents' association went to their local politicians and to the police, asking for help in trying to root this guy out and make their community safe again. But somehow Shields Corp found out about it. Their lawyer argued before city council that Langtry Glen had become an unsafe blight on the face of the city. Shields Corp convinced the city council to sell them the entire block from the city so they could raze the buildings and turn it into luxury condos."

She leaned back against the seat. "I was there the day Shields Corp dynamited the neighborhood.

The whole place was reduced to rubble in seconds. People cried. Shields Corp never even built on the property and just left it as an ugly vacant lot."

"You sound like you really hate Shields Corp."

"Wouldn't you? I imagine it's the opposite of everything TRUST stands for."

The road narrowed between two rocks again. Towering granite hemmed them in on both sides. Trees jutted out of the rocks above their heads. She shivered. Just moments ago the highway had stretched out to the horizon. The next it was all too claustrophobic. Was it her imagination, or did the towering pine sticking out ahead of them seem to be shaking? She forced a deep breath into her lungs and shut her eyes. Everything was going to be okay. Trees like that must have very strong root systems.

"Help us, Lord!" Mark shouted.

Her eyes jerked open to see a flash of green and brown as the tree hurtled down the cliff toward them.

SIX

Her body was thrown forward as Mark stomped on the brakes. The truck lurched sideways, spinning as he yanked on the steering wheel. There was the horrible sound of scratching against metal. Something smacked hard against her side of the truck. Then they slammed to a stop. Mark said something under his breath. She looked up.

The pine had missed the roof by inches. Katie tried to open her door, but it was wedged in the branches. Mark shoved his door open and jumped out. He walked around to the back of the truck, and she slid across the seat to follow him.

He held up a hand. "Hang on one sec. Something's wrong."

Well, yes. They were stuck under a tree. But even as she swung her legs out of the driver's side door, there was a warning note in his tone that made her pause. "Well?"

"This tree's been cut with a chainsaw." He kicked

at the trunk. "Looks like someone cut it most of the way through and then pushed it over."

"Into the road? But—"

Too late, she spotted Billy scrambling down the rock side. He leaped on top of Mark, his feet landing hard on Mark's shoulders. She screamed Mark's name as his body hit the ground. Billy stood over him, a black bandanna wrapped around his mouth, like a highwayman of old.

In an instant, Katie had jumped from the truck. But before she could even take a step, Billy pulled a gun from the waistband of his jeans. He pointed it at her head. "Get back in the truck or I'll kill him."

She climbed back into the seat.

"Now close the door, and don't turn around."

She shut the door, then slid the phone from her pocket and turned it on. No signal. And Mark's phone was clipped to his belt. She zipped the phone back into her inside pocket. Her eyes slid up to the rearview mirror, shivers shooting through her heart as she watched Mark stumble to his feet. His hands rose slowly and calmly in the air.

A sickening giggle slipped out of the teenager's mouth. He was high on something. She'd seen that dazed, unsteady look in Ethan's eyes enough times to recognize the signs. There was an emblem on his bandanna, too. It was yellow and green and oddly familiar. But she could only see a small portion of it. A gang sign? A terrorist group?

Billy cocked back the hammer. He set Mark in his sights.

Mark turned toward her. His eyes met hers in the mirror—steady, brave. Then he turned back to the boy with the gun, his lips moved as he whispered something under his breath and he knelt down in front of the fallen tree. It looked like he was praying. She began to pray. too. Desperate words tumbled through her mind in free fall.

Oh, God. Please. No. His life can't end like this. There has to be something I can do.

Her knee bumped against the key chain he'd left dangling from the ignition, and a single thought shot through her mind like a dart. One hand slid onto the gearshift. The other found the steering wheel. She grit her teeth and threw the truck in Reverse. The truck lurched backward. Billy spun around in fear as she braked inches from hitting them. Mark lunged at his attacker's knees, bringing Billy to the ground. She couldn't see what had happened to the gun.

Billy seemed to be swinging and hitting wildly, lashing out at Mark with everything he had. Mark was a stronger fighter, but she could also tell he was only trying to subdue the boy, not seriously injure him.

For a moment, the thought of jumping out to help flashed across her mind. But almost immediately she shoved it aside. She'd be more help by staying in the truck, especially if she could somehow position the vehicle so that Mark could climb back in.

Katie buckled her seat belt and reached for the gearshift. Too late she heard the passenger door slam and felt the paralyzing grip of a hand clamping around her wrist.

"Turn the truck around slowly, Katie," a menacing voice said very close to her ear, "or I will kill you and your friend."

It was Al.

Katie's breath froze in her chest. Her brain screamed silently in terror.

"Now you will do exactly as I say." There was a long, ugly knife in Al's hand. He brought it up slowly toward her throat and brushed the tip of the blade against her skin. She nodded dumbly and slid the truck into Drive.

Oh, God. Help me. Her heart pounded into her throat, threatening to choke her. Tears of panic pushed hard against her eyelids. Fear coursed through her veins like adrenaline. But she gritted her teeth until her jaw muscles ached and forced herself to focus, filling her thoughts with a single mantra, which blazed in her mind like a fire.

Stay calm. Stay in control. Stay alive.

She inched the truck forward, feeling the branches scrape against the truck as it moved. Her eyes went to the rearview mirror to see Mark and Billy still struggling on the ground.

"Drive!" Al averted his eyes for a moment to follow her gaze. The knife slipped down to her collar. Katie saw her chance.

Oh, God. Help me—

She hit the gas hard. The truck leaped forward.

"Slow down!"

She ignored him. The kidnapper tightened his grip on her arm, shouting mind-numbingly sadistic threats he'd exact on her if she didn't stop. She didn't stop. She could see Al's van now, ahead of her on the right, partially hidden behind a tree. She and Mark had driven past it without even seeing it or realizing they were heading into a trap.

Blocking everything out, Katie focused her attention on the rising speedometer in front of her. Just a little faster. Just a little farther.

The pain in her arm was increasing as Al pinned her right hand to her side. She couldn't see the knife. With a primeval scream, she yanked her arm away from his grasp and twisted the steering wheel as hard as she could. The truck spun wildly. Her seat belt snapped her back against the seat. Al was thrown violently against the passenger door. The knife fell to the floor.

The wheels locked. Tires skidded, screeching in protest. The truck slid off the road, flipping over onto its side as it fell into a drainage ditch. Katie's seat fell away beneath her. There was a bone-jarring jolt. Then everything stopped moving.

Suspended sideways in the top of the cab, Katie forced herself to breathe. She glanced down beside her and saw Al struggling to get his legs out from under the dashboard. In front of her, the windshield was a mess of splintering cracks. She let out a slow breath. At least it hadn't fallen inward.

Bracing one foot against the gearshift and her opposite knee against the drive column, she undid her seat belt. Then, clenching the door tightly, she grabbed for the steering wheel with the other hand and started to climb out through the open window. The truck had ended up one-hundred-and-eighty degrees, facing back toward where she'd left Mark struggling with his attacker. Billy was down on the ground now with Mark kneeling on top of him. But Mark was staring at her. His face was frozen in horror.

"Katie! I thought you—" The words choked in his throat.

"I'm fine." She climbed out. "Don't worry—"

Suddenly she felt a hand grab her foot, jerking her back toward the cab. She kicked out wildly and lost her balance. She fell out of the truck. Her head hit the dirt. Shadows rushed before her eyes filling her field of vision. The world went black.

SEVEN

The first thing Mark sensed were the vibrations shaking the hard, cold floor beneath him, filling his body with pain as he was jolted and jostled like a paper cup on a dryer. He tried to stretch but couldn't move. His mouth tasted like blood.

He opened his eyes. He was lying on the floor of the van. His hands were bound with duct tape. A strip of tape was stuck over his mouth.

Someone groaned behind him. Hope leaped in his chest. He rolled over, nearly bumping into Katie, lying on the floor behind him. Her eyes were closed. Her limbs were bound. Dried blood traced lines down the side of her face. But they were together, and she was alive.

Thank you, God.

When he'd seen Al dragging Katie's unconscious body down the road toward the van, the only thing that had mattered was stopping them from taking her—even if it meant losing his own life in the process. He'd rushed the vehicle and ended up with a bullet glancing off his thigh. Thankfully, Billy's aim was terrible. The wound wasn't even deep enough to need stitches, but it had been enough to make him stumble to his knees. That had been followed by a knock-out punch to the back of his head. His body was sore, but nothing felt broken.

He inched his body across the floor until he could feel her warmth against his chest. Her eyes blinked open, looking up into his. Huge and terrified. His heart lurched then filled with relief. At least they'd taken him, too.

Wrenching his eyes away from hers for a moment, he scanned the van, taking in as much information as he could. Billy was driving. Al seemed to be asleep in the passenger seat. Dense trees filled the view through the windshield. The road underneath them felt rough. The heavy rumble of the motor filled his ears. Okay, so they'd probably left the highway and were now on a back road.

He swallowed hard, forced the tension from his body and focused his eyes back on Katie's. Then, making sure she was watching, he began slowly and deliberately rubbing his shoulder against the strip of duct tape stuck down over his mouth, slowly easing the corner of it away from his lips. She nodded and followed suit. *Thank God for the eucalyptus cream.*

He never should have let himself be overpowered and caught off guard like this. Somehow he'd assumed that as long as they were together in his truck they'd be safe. If only he'd taken a safer route. Or insisted on police protection. Better yet, convinced her to drop the story altogether and return home to Toronto. But even the police hadn't predicted such a brazen daylight attack. Who were these people? Why were they after her? Did it really all link back to his father?

He worked away at the tape until he'd uncovered just the edge of his mouth, keeping his actions as small and slow as he could. If the kidnappers looked back, he didn't want them realizing what was going on. Katie did the same.

"You okay?" he whispered. Their faces were so close her nose was nearly brushing against his.

"I'm okay. You?"

"Yeah. I've got a thin bit of wire twisted around my belt loop..." Yet another trick he'd learned in his travels. "I'm going to use it to loosen the tape around my wrists. Then I'll show you how, okay?"

He began to rub his wrists against the wire until he'd torn a small strip down the center. Then he turned his wrists from side to side until the tape came loose. Right, now he could get his hands out anytime he wanted.

He untwisted the wire from his belt and wrapped it around the fingers of one hand. "Now, I need you to turn your back to me. I'm going to loosen the tape enough that you can get free. But leave the tape on, for now, okay?"

"Okay." She rolled away from him.

He glanced back toward the driver's seat. Billy still hadn't turned. Between the noise of the engine and the rattle of stones underneath them, chances were he'd practically have to shout for their kidnappers to hear him. The van was shaking so hard he probably wouldn't notice them rolling over, either. But still, every movement was a risk.

Mark rolled over, too, until they were back to back. His hands brushed against hers. They linked fingers. He gently worked the duct tape loose and then guided her on how to roll her wrists until she was free.

Oh, she had so much faith in him. He saw it in her eyes. Could she tell he didn't know how they were going to get out of this? That he was afraid of letting her down?

Once her hands were loose enough that she could slide out of the tape, they rolled back, face-to-face again, and lay there. Their eyes stayed locked on each other.

"Now what?" she breathed.

Good question. "Our best bet is to jump out before they get to wherever they're taking us. The problem's going to be picking a time when they can't just chase us down again. Normally, I'd say wait until we reach a traffic light, stop sign, gas station, something. But the bad news is that we're on a back road somewhere. They may not be stopping any-time soon."

If they jumped out while the van was moving, they'd end up pretty battered and bloody. There'd be nothing to stop Al and Billy from just chasing them down and throwing them back in the van again. Then they'd be in even less of a position to fight back.

The van dipped slightly. A flash of deep and dazzling blue water filled the windshield. There was the unmistakable sound of a metal bridge beneath the tires. Then the sky filled his vision again. Okay, so they'd just crossed over a lake, and judging by the sound of the bridge they were on a small, rural highway. But where?

Focus, Mark! You've had to find your bearings before. What else can you see?

The height of the sun in the sky told him it was almost noon. So they hadn't been driving much more than an hour. The angle of light reflected on the glass told him they were going northwest. So, they were still heading toward his dad's house. But on a small road that crossed a lake—

They crossed another bridge. Hope lit up inside his heart like fireworks. There was only one place he knew where the forest was this dense and the road twisted back and forth over the water—a broad expanse of conservation zone, about an hour's drive south of his family home.

"I know how we're going to get out of here." He said it louder than he'd intended to, his voice echoing back at him inside the tiny metal space. He winced and forced himself to lie still in case someone looked back. No one did. Her body slid closer to his.

"I think I know where we are," he whispered. "It's a pretty desolate wilderness area, but we can use that to our advantage. Can you swim?"

"Yeah."

"Great. The road crosses back and forth over the lake, which means that in a few minutes we're going to be crossing another bridge. When that happens, I'm going to yank the door open. When I do, I want you to rush toward the door as fast as you can and jump. Okay?"

She nodded. Again, there was that trust in her eyes, coupled with a strength and determination that humbled and spurred him on all at the same time. She leaned her head against his chest. He whispered a prayer into her hair and heard her echo "Amen."

"You're going to be right behind me, right?" she said.

"Right. Now, time to get free." He smoothly pulled his hands apart and then helped her separate hers. Of course, if Al or Billy looked back now they'd be sunk. But if his hunch was right, they'd just have to risk it. Katie tensed to spring.

Another flash of blue ahead. The van started over the bridge. "Now!"

The door flew back. She leaped, clearing the bridge and landing in the protection of the water beyond.

"Stop!" Billy shouted. He hit the brakes. The van swerved. Billy pulled the gun from his waistband. He waved it toward Mark, trying desperately to keep control of both weapon and vehicle. Al was awake now, fumbling with his seat belt. For a second, Mark glanced toward the fast-escaping freedom beyond the open door. Then he darted forward. One hand grabbed Billy's wildly flailing arm. The other pulled the bandanna off over the boy's head. It wasn't much of a clue to who their kidnappers were, but maybe authorities would recognize it.

Al had climbed out of his seat and was now trying to fit his bulk around the seat to get back to Mark. Al lunged and swung for his head. Mark blocked the blow with his forearm and then leveled a blow of his own into the large man's jaw. Al landed against Billy, knocking the teen's hands from the wheel as his head hit the windshield. The van spun out of control.

EIGHT

Mark threw himself out the open door. His body hit the bridge, rolled twice and tumbled into the water. He went under. But in two kicks he was back to the surface, just in time to see the van swerve over the other side of the bridge and plunge into the water below.

"You okay?" Katie was treading water a few feet away. She was clutching something in her hand, trying to hold it out of the water.

"Yeah. What have you got?"

"My phone." She sighed. "It was tucked inside my jacket, in a zip pocket. They must not have checked inside my clothes. It's so thin I didn't even realize it was there until I hit the water." The phone's case was smashed, almost like someone had stomped on it. Water was already seeping through the cracks in the casing. "It's destroyed."

"Don't be too hard on yourself," he said. "We wouldn't have been able to get a signal out here anyway. And I definitely wasn't thinking about checking my pockets the first time someone tried to abduct me." Considering the heart-stopping terror she must have been feeling, it was a wonder she'd had the self-awareness to even jump from the van. Most people he knew would still be lying there, paralyzed. "In fact, it was almost an hour after I escaped that first time before I calmed down enough to even realize I was bleeding. Do you still have your wallet?"

She shook her head.

"Me neither. Or my phone."

Even with the sun beating down, the water was cold enough to set his teeth chattering. "Come on, we've got to get out of here."

"But what about them?"

"The water's only about twelve feet deep. The van won't go all the way under."

They half swam, half walked a few more yards, keeping as close as they could to the water's edge, hidden in the reeds. But after they saw Billy and then Al crawl back onto the shore, they slipped into the forest and ran.

Sweat streamed down Mark's face. His body ached. His legs protested with every step. He could only imagine how Katie must be feeling.

For over an hour they'd picked their way through dense forest, scrubby brush, over hills and around swamps, never straying too far from the shoreline.

At first he'd paused every few minutes and listened for anyone pursuing them. But after the first half hour he'd stopped. Either their attackers hadn't seen where they'd gone or they'd been too thrown by the crash to try to follow them.

But they'd be out there, somewhere, waiting.

"If this is the lake I think it is, and I'm pretty much convinced of it by now, then we should hit the highway in about an hour or so."

Katie leaned against a tree, swung her head down between her knees. Tangled hair fell down around her dirt-streaked face, matted with sweat, blood and clinging mud. Her skirt hung in tatters around her knees, revealing a jagged maze of bloody cuts and scrapes covering her legs. He could still see the mark on her throat where Al had pressed in with the knife. She said, "But you think you've got a better idea."

Could she read him that easily?

"Yeah. The last thing I want is to just go walking down some rural highway alone, like a pair of ducks waiting to just be picked up again. My friend Zack is camping somewhere on this lake, and I'd feel safer if we concentrate on finding him."

Katie nodded slowly. Then she stood up straight, rolled her shoulders back and flashed a determined smile. "Then we do that."

She was incredible. He hadn't even heard her complain once. You'd have to have some kind of death wish to try attacking a girl like that. They started walking again, following the winding curves of the shoreline, scanning every cove for sign of a campsite.

Unlike a lot of people he'd met on his travels, Katie seemed quite comfortable walking in silence. He was grateful for that. An unsettling mixture of fear and guilt was pooling around the base of his spine. He needed to tell her that Jonah Shields was his father. Zack knew the truth of his identity. In fact, he used to work for his family.

The longer he went without telling her, the more betrayed she'd feel that he'd kept it from her. But he'd told himself to wait until she was safely dropped off at the hotel. So how could he just blurt something like that out now? They were in the middle of nowhere. They were still being hunted. If she lost her faith in him now, how could he continue to protect her?

Besides, for all he knew, the fact she didn't know he'd been born Jonah Shields Junior was the only reason they'd made it out of the van alive. If she had known, and somehow that had led to her kidnappers finding out, there was no telling what they'd have done.

His dad had made a lot of enemies. While most had taken up the fight against Shields Corp through legal channels, there was always that tiny, radical fringe element who were willing to resort to violent, illegal means to get their point across.

He didn't still didn't know how one reporter fit into this. But if Al and Billy were targeting her to get to his father, how much more would it have put Katie's life at risk if they knew she was traveling with Jonah Shields's only son? Would they have even bothered leaving her alive once they knew what they had? Or would they have just left her bloody body at the side of the highway while they used him to get whatever they wanted from his father?

He shuddered. A disgruntled former employee had tried to kidnap his sister when she was six. After a desperate half-hour search, Shields's security had found the terrified child tied up in the car trunk of someone who was trying to leave the property. Sunny had never gone anywhere without security since.

He'd been ten at the time and determined not to have security detail. He'd made a sport out of dodging whoever his father's company tried assigning to watch him—leading them on wild-goose chases to find him while he hid on the roof of the family home, watching them all scurry below.

But when he was twelve, Zack had landed in his life. Hired by his grandmother, not his father. Only seven years older than his rebellious assignment, Zack was a private in the infantry on standby for overseas deployment. The very first thing he'd done with young Mark was taken him camping, in these very woods, miles away from the sheltered walls in which he'd grown up. When Mark had run away from his tent in the middle of the night, Zack had just quietly and patiently tracked him until, exhausted and utterly lost, Mark had given up, turned around and discovered the man he was running from had never been more than a few yards behind, quietly looking out for him.

"The first rule of running," Zack had told him, "is to figure out where you're running to."

So what would he think of the fact Mark still hadn't told Katie the truth about his past?

"There!" Mark pointed across the river "That's Zack's camp."

Katie followed his finger. She couldn't see anything but a mass of trees and rocks, identical to every other tree and rock she'd seen all day. It felt as though they'd been walking for hours. She didn't know what was worse—knowing there was someone out there trying to hurt her or feeling so completely dependent on this good-looking stranger for help.

Not that she wasn't thankful. Of course, she was insanely grateful that Mark had been there last night on the train tracks and that she hadn't tried to drive up to Kapuskasing alone. It wasn't like she didn't trust him.

But trusting someone wasn't the same as feeling comfortable relying on them to keep saving you.

Ever since she'd arrived at the train station things had kept happening that were beyond her control.

When you depended on someone else you made yourself weak enough to let them hurt you. The thought of losing her independence under the thumb of a strong-willed man—like her mother, like her sister had—terrified her. That was never going to happen.

Yes, there was something about being around Mark that made her feel safe. He made her feel like he was worth entrusting her life to. Like she'd be safe in his hands. That scared her even more. If she ever let her guard down enough to fall completely and totally in love with a man like that, her heart would be more vulnerable than she could bear. And then what if he violated that trust? She could lose her independence forever. He was still pointing at nothing. "You see it?"

"No."

His hand brushed over her shoulder as he turned her toward one particular cove. She concentrated on the opposite shoreline of trees like a puzzle she wasn't about to admit she couldn't solve. Then she saw it—a pattern of green and brown that didn't quite match the trees around it and the faint haze in the air of campfire smoke. "Yeah, I can see it."

"Do you think you can swim to it?"

"Absolutely." At least her punishing schedule at work hadn't stopped from her going on nightly runs to burn off stress. She didn't know how she'd handle it if she actually had to rely on him to drag her across the lake.

Mark pulled his shoes and socks off and then rolled up the legs of his jeans over his knees. His calves were as strong and lean as a marathon runner's. "If you give me your shoes, I'll carry them with mine."

Then he pulled his T-shirt off over his head, and her eyes unconsciously slipped to the breadth of his shoulders, the muscle of his arms and the wild, untamed strength of his chest. Forget fearing men like her stepfather and brother-in-law. A man like this could fell them in a single blow.

He dropped their shoes, socks and Katie's damaged cell phone into his T-shirt. He tied the ends together like a pack. Then he pulled a black bandanna from his jean pocket, rolled it tightly into a thin roll and tied it to the bundle. Laying the pack across his back, he tied the bandanna across his chest diagonally, looping it over one shoulder and under the other arm. Keeping his hands free for swimming.

Katie stared at the bright green-and-yellow pattern crossing the very center of his chest. It was the same as the one Billy had been wearing.

She stepped back. "Where did you get that?"

"What?" He followed her gaze. "Oh, this? I ripped it off that kid's neck just before the van crashed. I thought it might give us some clue to who they were or what they were after."

Her heart started beating again. Of course. If she'd been thinking straight, she probably would've grabbed it herself. She followed him down to the water's edge and, when he paused to let her go ahead, dove in.

Cold water struck her skin like the flat edge of a knife blade. She gritted her teeth, plunged beneath the surface and swam a few strokes before coming up for air.

The reason Mark had the bandanna made sense. Of course, if her phone still worked she could've sent a picture of the logo back to Chad at *Impact News* and have him research it for her. If she'd had her computer, she could've researched it herself.

That's when it hit her—she didn't even have her wallet anymore. Her identification, her belongings, her way of communicating with the outside world— they'd all been stripped away from her.

There was a splash. Then Mark was beside her, swimming steadily, matching her stroke for stroke.

She'd never been so helpless. She'd never felt so safe.

NINE

A stocky man was waiting for them when they scrambled to shore. There was a hint of gray at the edge of his cropped hair. The smile on his face was genuine, but Katie could see a definite concern reflected in his eyes. "I thought I wasn't seeing you until Monday."

Mark crawled up onto the beach and sat down, gasping for breath.

"There...was..." He gulped hard. "Man, we're in trouble."

Her bare feet brushed against the ground. Zack waded in toward her, his face still trained on Mark.

"What kind of trouble? Is this related to your—" But the words froze in Zack's mouth, as Mark waved a hand to silence him.

"Your...wha—" she started. She gasped in a painful breath as her voice failed her. She watched in helpless frustration as the two men exchanged looks.

What wasn't Mark telling her?

Reaching her, Zack scanned her face. "I'm Zack.

May I help you ashore?" She nodded weakly. He slipped an arm under her shoulder and walked her to land. "Are you hurt?"

Again, the question was directed at her. She would have laughed if she'd had the strength. Her whole body was scraped and bruised, shivering from the cold water and aching from fatigue. But he'd already know that.

Again, she shook her head. Zack glanced to Mark. "You?"

Mark also shook his head. "We're…kind of…battered. But nothing strained…or broken."

Zack led her to a camp chair in front of a fire, helped her sit and then dropped a blanket around her shoulders. He rustled around in a cooler for a moment, coming up with an energy drink and granola bar, which he pressed into her hands. "Eat and drink slowly. Tiny bites."

Mark stumbled up to the fire. "Thanks. Someone has been…pursuing us." He gasped. "I don't know… who they are."

Zack passed him a blanket. "Rest. Eat. Then tell me."

Mark pulled his arm out from the bandanna. He tossed it to Zack, who carefully untied it from the makeshift T-shirt bundle holding the shoes and phone.

Zack held the bandanna up and ran his eyes over the logo. "What is this?"

"One of the kidnappers was wearing it." Mark sat on a rock. "Seen it before?"

Zack's frown deepened. "No. It doesn't look like any terrorist or organized crime group I've ever seen."

"May I?" Katie took it, turned it upside down and stretched it out on her lap, her eyes tracing over the swath of green, punctuated by spikes of yellow. Her heart sank. "This is the logo of the Langtry Glen Residents Association. I thought it was vaguely familiar before, but I didn't recognize it until it was rolled flat." She took a deep breath and was glad to find her voice had returned. She looked through the campfire at Mark. Then she turned to Zack.

"I'm a newspaper reporter for *Impact News*," she said. "I came up here to cover a party held by the same real-estate developer who destroyed their community. They had these made up when they heard they'd lost the fight to keep their buildings and handed them out to supporters who'd come to watch their buildings get demolished. People cried when the detonations went off." She turned to Mark. "I don't understand. A few people posted some angry comments on our website, accusing me of having forgotten Langtry Glen. But that's worlds away from actually sending someone up here to kidnap me."

"You said that a drug dealer had been using the

community as a base," Mark said. "Is it possible that someone from that community had explosives training?"

"You're kidding, right? I was referring to the regular dynamiting the developer did. The buildings were demolished in seconds. But Langtry Glen itself was just a normal apartment complex—full of good, decent people who had fallen on hard times. It's far more likely that someone is setting them up."

But the grim look on Mark's face told her he was anything but joking. He turned to Zack. "Someone wearing this bandanna ambushed us at the side of the road. It was the second serious attempt they'd made to kidnap Katie, and this time they got all of my equipment, including the radio transmitter."

Zack sucked in a harsh breath. A sudden burst of guilt filled her heart. She'd been so busy focusing on their escape she hadn't even realized he'd left his equipment behind.

Mark turned to Katie. "The reason I asked about explosives is that I left the unit unlocked. Anyone can just open it up and use it."

"But it's just a radio studio and transmitter."

"A transmitter is like any other tool. In the right hands, it can save a lot of lives, but in the wrong hands, it's potentially deadly. In this case, radio transmitters can be used in bomb-making. Just like a cell phone, but without relying on an external carrier to relay the signal. All bombs have some form of detonation mechanism. When it comes to homemade explosives, that usually means either using some form of a countdown timer or, better still, a remote detonator that can send a signal to the bomb when you're safely out of the area."

She nodded. "Like how you can use a car door opener to set off an explosive?"

"Exactly. It's the transmitter itself that sends the signal, and normally long-range radio transmitters are hard to find. Let alone portable ones. So for your average terrorist group it wouldn't be worth the trouble of figuring out how to build one. But a fully integrated, long-range radio transmitter with timing capability..." He groaned. "I know it's a long-shot. But when you mentioned building demolition, it reminded me of how much damage my transmitter could do in the wrong hands."

"Although," Zack said, "we have no reason to believe that it will be."

"But I also had no reason to believe someone would try to kidnap me," Katie said.

Zack's forehead wrinkled. "You're sure it's you they're after?"

"Absolutely. One of them followed me up from Toronto. The other was waiting for me at Cobalt train station. Fortunately, Mark happened to be there." She swallowed hard.

"I'd offered to give her a ride to her hotel," Mark

added. "They attacked us on the road. They had weapons and managed to get us into the back of their van." Zack's face paled. "We jumped out when they cut through the nature preserve. I decided the safest course of action was coming to you. For all we knew they'd be patrolling the roads."

"And we now think this is somehow tied back to the destruction of some low-income housing?" Zack directed the question at Katie.

"Langtry Glen was acquired and then destroyed by Shields Corp," Mark said. "Jonah Shields is holding a weekend gala of sorts tomorrow. Must be big if he's inviting the press all the way up from Toronto."

There was an edge to his voice that she couldn't quite place. The two men were staring at each other right in the eyes, like two old-fashioned gunslingers waiting to see who would flinch first.

What didn't she know?

She pushed the blanket down onto her lap, shook her wet hair out around her shoulders and fixed her eyes on Mark.

"There's something you're not telling me," she said softly but firmly.

He didn't flinch. "It's nothing you need to know right now."

It was the tone of a man used to taking charge. Just like the tone she'd heard both her stepfather and brother-in-law use before. For him to take charge when she was running for her life was one thing.

But to control what she was allowed to know? He wasn't looking at her.

"I'm trusting you."

"And I'm just trying to keep you safe."

"Well, I'd feel a whole lot safer knowing that we're being totally hon—" But the word froze on her tongue as his eyes looked up into hers, and she saw the intensity of emotion echoed there. This wasn't the look of a man who was trying to dismiss her. If anything, he looked even more worried than she was.

Mark stood up and walked around the campfire. His eyes trained firmly on her face. Zack quietly slipped into the tent.

Mark crouched down in the sand beside her. His placed his hand on the arm of her chair, inches away from hers. "I read some of your newspaper articles online this morning." She frowned. His fingers brushed against her arm. "No, I mean the good ones. The older ones you published before Ethan took over as editor. Took some digging, but I was able to find a few archived. You're really very good."

A slight flush rose to her cheeks as a gentle warmth spread through her chest. But almost instantly she brushed the feeling aside. She was pleased he liked her work, maybe even a little more pleased than she'd expected to be. But she didn't need his approval. She needed the truth.

"You write with both brains and heart." He paused

and forced his hand through his hair like he was trying to find the right words. "Like you don't just care about facts but also about people. Haven't you ever found yourself holding something back when you write a story? Not lying, just omitting a few details because they were irrelevant and could hurt someone? Or even not asking someone a question because you knew the line of questioning was needlessly painful or uncomfortable?"

Of course she had. Especially in cases of sexual assault, child abuse or the death of a loved one. True, other journalists might be willing to reduce someone to tears for a story. But something inside her—her faith, she hoped—had always made her conscious of respecting the person she was interviewing.

She nodded. "Yes. But the people I interview also know they can trust me with the truth."

Mark looked away.

"Hey, you'll never guess what I've got." Zack was standing in the doorway of the tent with a battered rucksack in his hand. He tossed it to Mark.

"You found it." Mark stood. "I left this bag somewhere when I was in Kandahar last month. Zack here said he'd find it for me." He pulled out a pair of simple khakis and a faded blue T-shirt and held them out toward her. "I'm sorry these will be a bit big. But at least they're clean."

"Thank you." While a skirt and jacket had seemed the perfect mix of professional and casual when she's gotten up this morning, now they were tattered, soaked and streaked with mud. She ran her eyes out over the wide expanse of lake and the thick trees surrounding them. Zack had to have gotten here somehow. "What's our next move? I'm guessing you don't have a phone?"

Zack shook his head. "No, sorry. I'm totally unplugged. No phone. No internet. Nada."

She stood. "How far to the closest police station? Are we walking, or do you have a vehicle we can borrow?"

Zack's brows raised slightly. Again his eyes flickered over to Mark. Questioning. Mark shrugged.

"I have a motorcycle, which you're welcome to borrow. I was planning on picking Mark up on it, so I've already got a second seat on and two helmets. Timmins is about an hour on bike from here. I left a first aid kit out on my sleeping bag. There's fresh water in there, too. How about you get yourselves turned around and I'll sort out some lunch before you go?"

Yeah, as much as she was in a hurry to go, he was probably right.

"Thanks." She slipped into the cool darkness of the tent, letting the thick canvas close behind her. She dropped onto Zack's rollout cot and let her head fall between her knees again.

Deep breath in. Deep breath out. Come on, Katie. Don't fall apart now.

For a moment, she tried to remember the words of the psalm Celia had given her. But as the words slipped across her mind, she found her own frustration seeping through.

Dear God, if you really know what's going on here, can you let me know? Please. Because the more I'm doubting whether I should be trusting Mark, the harder I'm finding to trust that this is all going to turn out okay.

The soft cotton fabric smelled like Mark. Warm, comforting, strong, wild. She closed her eyes, remembering the feel of his fingers against hers as he'd helped her cut her wrists free. She blinked hard and tossed the clothes on the cot.

Come on, Katie. Get a grip. She didn't need a man who could keep her safe. She needed someone she could be sure would never be able to hurt her. Mark was nothing like what she thought she wanted. Yet somehow he'd been capable of stepping in to be everything she'd needed him to be. She pressed her fingers into her temples.

Trust your instincts, Katie. Always trust your instincts.

But which ones? Her old, reliable ones, which told her to always ask questions and dig deeper—the ones who were always safest knowing the whole story? Or these new, scarier ones, which just wanted to send her falling into the safety of his arms?

* * *

Zack poked the fire with a stick, turning over the coals until the flame flickered brighter. "Wow, she's something else." His voice was so low it was almost a whisper. Mark guessed, tailored to be loud enough he could hear without risking them being overheard. "I take it she's also romantically unattached?"

"Don't even go there." Mark scowled and dropped down in the camp chair she'd just vacated. Yes, Katie was incredible. Not just beautiful as a woman but impressive as a human being. It was hardly surprising his friend had noticed. So why was he so annoyed by it? "Katie deserves far better than some unavailable man who goes jetting around the world at a moment's notice."

"I'm not scheduled to deploy for another nine weeks...."

Mark's eyes shot toward the sky in irritation.

Zack chuckled quietly. "Oh, don't worry. I've recently struck up a very promising friendship with someone back at base. But it's nice to see you so interested in someone for once."

"I'm not interested. I'm protective. She needs me. I'm just getting her where she needs to be." That was all it was. That was all it could be.

Zack leaned forward, resting his forearms on his knees. "Which happens to be your family? Although I'm taking it by all the dirty looks and hushing earlier she doesn't know they're your family."

This was exactly why he hadn't wanted to tell Zack about meeting with his father—not that he expected to be making that meeting now. It had been over ten years since he'd stepped down from being Mark's bodyguard, but sometimes that old dynamic didn't feel that far under the surface. "It's safer that she doesn't know—"

"For her or for you?"

"For us both!" His voice echoed loud in the quiet. He caught himself and lowered it again. "People are trying to kidnap her. Probably for reasons related to my family. If they find out she's with me, that might double the danger she's in. Even her knowing could put her life in greater danger—"

"Why?"

"What if she flips out and runs away? What if she won't let me protect her?"

"You mean what if she rejects you?"

Mark shoved his palms onto his knees and stood up quickly, sending the camp chair flying. "I can't have this conversation right now. Not while Katie's in danger."

He'd taken three steps down the beach before Zack's words made him stop. "Well, I could always take her to the police station instead. You can stay here and get an early start on your holiday."

"I'm canceling my vacation." Mark turned back. "I'm flying to Lebanon in three days. Then Zimbabwe. Then Romania. I'll be gone for six months.

Maybe more. So I'll see her off safely today, be back here tomorrow night, then Sunday I'll need you to drop me at a bus station." He sighed. "So you see, even if I wanted to pursue a relationship with Katie, it couldn't happen. And anything that did happen between us would be a mistake. At best, an open-ended long-distance relationship with no hope of ever actually being together. And at worst she'd be…" His voice trailed off.

Zack chuckled again and went back to poking the fire. Tension gripped Mark's shoulders, and for a moment he was tempted to pick up something and throw it. Nothing about this was funny.

"Just drop it, okay?" Mark's voice rose. "What I was going to say was *fling*. That's what Katie would be to me—a fling. You don't think we both deserve better than that?"

The smile dropped from Zack's face. He waved his hand downward as though trying to lower the temperature. "You might want to—"

"To what? Look, Katie is amazing." He was practically shouting. "But I'm not about to burden her with the truth about my life. We don't have a future together. Not with her as a partner. Not with her as a wife. She's just someone who landed in my lap, who needed to be rescued, nothing more."

Zack raised a finger to his lips in warning. The tent flap flew open. Katie stepped out. Her face was so calm and composed that for a moment he hoped she hadn't heard his outburst. Then he saw the tiny tremor in her lower lip and realized just how tightly she was pressing her lips together. Noticed the polite, self-controlled mask that had snapped over her eyes in place of real, heartfelt emotion. His heart sunk like a stone. She'd heard enough.

For one gut-wrenching moment, his eyes still searched her face, looking for a chink in her emotional armor. If he could just catch a flash of anger or a glimmer of hurt, he'd know how to respond. He'd be able to figure out how to rush in with the right word to say and save her from the pain. He'd be able to fix this—to go from villain to hero. She walked over to the fallen chair, picked it up and sat down. Mark grabbed the rucksack and strode down the beach.

TEN

Katie watched the flames flicker and dance and focused on pushing the overheard snatches of conversation out of her mind. So what if he couldn't see himself having a future with her? She couldn't afford to think about that now. Judging by the arc of the sun in the sky, the afternoon was quickly disappearing. Chances were she'd miss the media briefing and have to play catch-up tomorrow. Not to mention reporting her stolen wallet, replacing her belongings, finding a hotel room, explaining to work why she'd been off the grid all day. She sighed. Ethan had better be in one of his more understanding moods.

Zack walked over to his metal food box and pulled out some cans. He came back, sat in front of the fire and slowly spooned a tin of beans into a metal pot. He did the same with a tin of meat and then another of tomatoes. Then he mixed them all together in the pot and stirred it over the campfire. His motions were slow, deliberate, relaxed. Whereas here she was practically ready to pelt down the beach and sprint through the woods if it would get her life back on track any faster. A thousand unasked questions clattered in her mind. But something told her he wasn't about to tell her anything she wanted to know.

Finally she said, "How well do you know Mark?"

The spoon paused but only briefly. "About as well as anybody does, I reckon."

"You care about him, don't you?"

Zack's jaw tightened ever so slightly. "He's like a brother to me."

Yeah, she could see that. "I'm not going to ask you to break his confidence. But he's obviously keeping something from me. Something he doesn't trust me with…" *Was that why he'd said she could never be anything more than a fling?* Sudden tears rushed to her eyes. She swallowed hard. "What am I supposed to do?"

Zack's eyes met hers again. They were as gray and unflinching as steel. "Trust him, Katie. Trust him with your life."

She breathed a sigh of relief when Mark came jogging back, dressed in clean jeans and a simple navy shirt. He nodded politely, then sat on the other side of the fire, his thoughts lost far beyond her reach. Lunch was simple but filling. Zack had only one set of dishes. So he divided the chili between a plate, a bowl and the pot, and they used slices of bread to spoon it into their mouths. Then they washed the meal down with water from Zack's canteen.

She sat down on the beach, watching the sun glisten off the water as she listened to Mark and Zack pore over a map. The plan was to cut straight through the woods, due north, until they hit a road. Then they'd head west. A breeze rustled in the trees around her. She closed her eyes and lay back. It had been years since she'd been anywhere this peaceful. The thought hit her with a jolt—if everything had gone as planned, she would never have seen any of it. She'd have never met Mark or even stopped in Cobalt. Rather, she would have just gone from the concrete jungle of the city, to the train, to a hotel, to the event at the Shieldses' without even pausing for breath.

Was that what it took to make her slow down? A knife to her throat? Her life in danger?

She couldn't remember the last time she'd gone this long without checking her phone. She'd tried drying it out by burying it in a bowl of dry rice from Zack's food supplies. Surprisingly, the power button had begun glowing again, but when she turned it on the screen remained blank. The remains were now back in her pocket. Hopefully, she could at least transfer its memory and data to a new phone.

"Did I tell you I own a really small island?"

She opened her eyes.

Mark was kneeling beside her. "It's on a lake like

this. Not all that far from here." He looked out over the water, the dark blue echoing back in the green of his eyes. "It's really, really tiny. I used to think I was going to build a house on it. Move up here. But it's never going to happen."

"Why are you telling me this?" She pulled herself up to sitting.

"Because it's something nobody else really knows about me. And because I actually do want you to know me better. I just don't know where or how to start."

So a peace offering then. One private tidbit of information to make up for everything he wasn't telling her.

Mark stood slowly and stretched out his hand to take hers. But when she shook her head, he stuffed it into his pocket and stood back. "You heard me arguing with Zack, didn't you?"

"Yes." She climbed to her feet. "We're in this together, Mark. I have to trust you. You have to trust me, too."

He closed his eyes like he was listening to an argument inside his head. Then he opened them again, filled with look of such regret that for a moment she wished she could just let herself hug him. "You're right. You deserve the complete truth. All of it. Just not here, okay? Not like this. Let me get you safely to the police and put a call in to my partner, Nick. Then tonight, how about I take you out for dinner, somewhere quiet and private and then—" he took a deep breath "—I'll tell you everything. You can decide what you want to do from there. Until then, I'm just hoping you can trust me. Is that all right with you?"

Not really, but it wasn't like she was brimming with options. "Okay. I'll drop it until then. But tonight, you tell me everything. Before the sun sets tonight." She reached for his hand. "Promise?"

He reached for her hand, enveloping her fingers in his. He shook her hand solemnly. "I promise. Now come on. I want to show you how Zack hides his bike."

She followed him a few yards down the beach until they reached what looked like a random mass of brush. Reaching in, Mark grabbed the bush with both hands and pulled. A camouflage tarp peeled away, showing a powerful off-road motorcycle underneath.

She laughed. "That's a neat trick."

He rolled up the tarp, cleanly folding away the fake branches.

"Mark made it for me." Zack was striding up the beach. "The man's a total genius." He eased the bike out of its hiding place. "Now, you're going to want to head down the beach about thirty yards. Then you'll see a gap in the trees on your left. It's a moose track, I think. I've used it before. You should have no problem."

Mark clasped Zack on the shoulder. "Thanks

again. You're a lifesaver. I'll come back for you to-morrow."

"No hurry. Just take care of Katie, and come back whenever you can. I just wish I'd brought my firearm with me. I hate the idea of sending you off unarmed."

Mark swung his leg easily over the motorcycle. Then he reached for Katie's hand and pulled her up behind him. "It's okay. My firearm license was in my wallet anyway, and I don't think the police would take too kindly to an unidentified armed man cruising down the highway."

Zack reached into his pocket and pulled out a couple of twenties and a prepaid credit card. "Take this. You'll have enough gas to make it to the highway. But you may have to stop to fuel up on the way and you'll both probably have some other expenses until you can sort your stuff out."

"Thanks, man. I'll pay you back."

"I know you will."

Mark reached out to take the borrowed money. But Zack grabbed him by the arm instead. The money fell onto the sand as Zack pulled Mark's arm in for a closer look at the leather strap encircling his wrist. "Hold on. If this is what I think it is, this could be a total game changer."

Five minutes later, they were sitting back at the campfire while Zack turned the GPS medallion over in his hands.

"I'm telling you," Mark said, "it's been deactivated. I scanned it thoroughly when I got it, and it wasn't emitting any signal."

Zack's brow furrowed. "But there used to be a way of reactivating it. If so, I might even be able to trigger the emergency beacon."

Emergency beacon? Katie looked from one man to the other. The idea of someone giving their grandson a medallion with a tracking GPS in it was rare but not unheard of. There were a host of stylish GPS options for people traveling in dangerous countries or who wanted to ensure their kid's safety. Some companies installed a GPS in their employees' cell phones or cars—though the ones that weren't up-front about it tended to face stiff fines for violating the right to privacy. But an emergency beacon?

Zack disappeared into his tent and reappeared with a metal twist tie. Carefully, he stripped the plastic off, revealing the long, thin wire underneath. "May I?"

Mark nodded. Zack split the wire in two and then bent each wire in half. He stuck the pieces into tiny holes on each side of the medallion. Mark slid over beside Katie. His forearm brushed against hers, as if he wanted to take her hand but wasn't sure if he should.

"Why did your grandmother give you an emergency beacon?" she whispered.

"She was afraid someone might try to kidnap me. My family history is a mess. Someone kidnapped my sister when I was little, and although we got her back okay, she never really recovered."

Katie's hand rose to her throat. "I'm so sorry. But why…"

Mark's eyes met hers. Pleading with her to trust him just one last time. "Tonight. Before the sun sets. I will tell you everything—every horrible, sordid detail about my family and my past—"

She slid her fingers between his and squeezed. "Tonight."

Zack jumped to his feet. "Got it. The GPS is now active again. Although I have no idea if anyone would be monitoring the signal now, I can program the signal into my GPS tracker so that at least I will know where you are." Then he frowned. "I don't remember how to activate the emergency beacon though."

"You grab both sides of the medallion at once and twist it," Mark said slowly, like he was reciting something from a long forgotten instruction manual. "It's the same motion as if you were trying to unscrew a jar lid. There's a connector in the middle, and if the seal breaks, the beacon emits an alarm. Or at least it used to."

Katie's fingers tightened in his. "What happens if the alarm goes off?"

"Honestly? I have no idea."

* * *

It was like flying without an airplane. Katie tightened her arms around Mark's waist and stifled a gasp as the bike shot through the forest. Huge wheels skimmed along the ground. The track wound harshly: left, right, left, right. Rocks, trees, lakes, sky blended into a blur rushing past her eyes. The heavy thrum of the motorcycle engine filled her ears.

Trust him, Katie. Trust him with your life.

What choice did she have? Sure, when they reached the police station there would be statements to give, decisions to be made, work to be done. Not to mention she'd have an undoubtedly infuriated Ethan to contact and calm.

When the engine stopped, when she stepped down off that bike she would need to be in control again. She would be the one grabbing the handlebars and forcing her life forward in the way it needed to go.

But as for this moment, she was out of control. She was the passenger, holding on to Mark as he drove her forward at his speed with his hand on the throttle. Leaving her with nothing to do but hold on to him and gasp.

The dirt path widened. They skimmed along a road by the water's edge, dodging between the rocks and holes like a skipping stone. The pale blue expanse of endless sky filled her eyes.

Trust him.

She closed her eyes and leaned her body against the warmth of his back, feeling the motorcycle vibrations move through his body into hers. She cleared her mind until, one by one, the host of clamoring voices who filled her brain with their incessant demands for attention were drowned out by roar of the wind rushing up around her and the steady beat of the bike pulsing through her. And still the bike rode on.

They shot out of the forest and onto the paved expanse of a straight, modern highway. For a moment, she thought she could see an old log trading house ahead on her right and then realized it was relatively modern gas station and souvenir store. A large wooden bear out front held a sign encouraging them to try their luck at the mini-golf course in the back. But the place seemed deserted, darkness filling the empty space between the gingham curtains and window boxes.

Mark eased on the gas and pulled in. He cut the engine. Silence hit her like a wave as the pulsing noise of the engine disappeared, leaving nothing but the gentle hush of wind floating through the trees around them. He pulled off his helmet and ran his fingers through his sweat-soaked hair.

She unclasped her helmet and pulled it off. Mark reached up to sweep a lock of hair off her face. "You okay?"

She nodded, feeling his fingers moving gently along her face. "That was unbelievable."

"Not too fast?"

She shook her head.

Sliding his hand away from her slowly, Mark took a step back and let out a long, deep breath. "You really are something else." He'd said it so quietly Katie was left wondering if she'd really heard him.

Mark looked around at the empty parking lot then glanced down at his watch. "We're still about twenty minutes from Timmins. But we're running pretty low on gas, so I thought I'd better stop and fill up."

She slid off the bike. "This place looks closed."

"It is. But they have a pay pump. Just give me a few minutes, and we'll be back on our way."

Nodding faintly, Katie glanced along to where the sun was beginning its slow journey back down toward the tree line. The afternoon was disappearing.

Then Mark stepped toward her. As the sun fell across his back, the shadows on his face looked deeper, his eyes darker. "I told Zack I'd return the bike tomorrow. But tonight I'm going to book a room in the same hotel you do. If they've got space." He chuckled. "If they don't, I guess I'll camp out in the lobby. Just to make sure you're not alone. Just to be there in case anything… I mean, I just couldn't…" He reached for her, sliding his arms around her waist. The rough skin on his cheek brushed against her face. "The whole bike ride here, I kept trying to wrap my head around my logical next moves. But all I could think about was how badly it was going to kill me to say goodbye to you tomorrow."

He stroked his fingers along the top of her head, down her neck and along her spine until they found the soft dip in the small of her back. He pulled her closer to him, deepening their hug. He leaned forward until his lips brushed against her forehead. "It just feels too soon to say goodbye. Now that I've met you, how can I just walk away without knowing I did everything I possibly could to protect you, to keep you...safe?"

Her hands slipped up around his neck, brushing her fingertips along the soft hair at the nape of his neck. His breath quickened. Her eyes closed. *"We don't have a future together. Not with her as a partner. Not with her as a wife. She's just someone who landed in my lap, who needed to be rescued, nothing more."*

"I never asked you to protect me." Like a diver breaking through the ice, Katie wrenched herself away from him. "I heard what you told Zack." Hot tears threatened to spill from underneath her lids. "How I was just someone needing rescuing. Nothing more."

Raising both her hands to his chest, she gently pushed him away. But her will almost faltered when she saw the strength and intensity building in his eyes. "I am not some lost kitten that needs to be rescued. I don't need you to shelter me, or protect me, or follow me around, wrap me up in cotton wool to make sure I'm okay. I'm always going to be thankful you were there for me. I owe you my life and I know it. But you don't really know me, and I...I don't know who you are, either."

He stepped back. "I'm sorry for what I said to Zack. I didn't mean it the way it sounded." He let out a long breath. "You're right. You're incredibly strong. Plus you're gutsy. The way you handled everything that's happened has just been incredible, and yeah, I'm sure when you're in your element and kidnappers aren't breathing down your neck you're a serious force to be reckoned with."

"Then let me show you that side of me, too," she said. "Stay up here this weekend. Come with me on my assignment. Be my date for the Shields gala. Watch me do my job. It will give you a chance to see what I'm really like when I'm not busy running or ducking for cover."

He ran his hand over his head. "Actually, I was kind of hoping I might be able to change your mind about covering that event."

"You must be joking." She stepped back. "I can't just start turning down assignments. Ethan would fire me on the spot."

"Well, I'm hoping that after we talk tonight you'll feel differently."

"I'm positive I won't. Mark, I've been really understanding about whatever this business is that's going on with you. I've respected the fact you wanted to keep some things private. But nothing you could possibly say is going to stop me from doing my job. I need my job. I love what I do. It's who I am."

A hard, unexpected look flashed across Mark's face as though he were smiling at a joke that wasn't very funny. For a moment, she could feel her breath catch inside her chest, as his arms began to slide away as if to make a space for her between them. But then he wrenched his eyes away again. "You're right. I need to respect that your life matters to you, too." He rolled his shoulders back. "I've got to go fill up the tank. I suggest you walk around a bit before we keep going. Your legs can get pretty cramped on the back of a bike."

She paused, uncertain. But he had already turned away. Katie sighed and followed the direction the bear was pointing.

Katie wandered around the empty mini-golf course. Plastic beavers chased painted fish around the first hole. A chorus of wolves was poised to howl around the third. A dormant waterfall stood by the end of the course. She pulled a rust-stained putter from its base and gave it an experimental swing.

She'd never planned for her life to be like this. As a teenager, she pictured herself not only finding work that she loved but also getting married, raising a family, going to church on Sunday mornings, having some form of balance in her life. Instead, it felt like she'd traded in everything else of value to work a job that left her feeling worse at the end of the day.

A breeze tickled the trees. Psalm 139 flickered at the edge of her mind again. The actual piece of paper Celia had given her had been lost somewhere between getting ambushed on the road and trekking to Zack's campsite. But many of the words had stayed with her.

Oh God, you have searched me, and you know me. You perceive my thoughts from afar...

This is not what I planned, God. None of this. Is any of this part of your plan?

Mark kicked the tires of the dirt bike. Then he walked the bike around to the automatic air pump at the back of the building. The tire pressure was actually pretty good, but it never hurt to be careful. A wry smile curved at the corner of his lips—he'd take almost any excuse to delay the inevitable for a few more moments.

"Hey, God," he said, under his breath, "I know I asked you once to find me the right woman. But she wasn't supposed to show up until my company was in a stronger position. And she was definitely not supposed to be a journalist, let alone one on her way to see my family."

He ran his hand along the back of his neck. The muscles were tight.

Tonight. He'd promised to tell her tonight. And he would. Before she had the chance to stumble upon a picture of him at his father's party and recognize the man he was now in the eyes of the boy he used to be. Would she understand and forgive him? Or would she feel betrayed? Presume he was just like his father? Count off the number of chances he'd had to tell her the truth since they'd met on the railway tracks last night? Never want to see him again?

He closed his eyes so tightly his lids ached. No matter what he said, she'd be determined to do her job. She hadn't worked all this time at a shot at editorship just to let the chance encounter with him steal it all away from her. He couldn't put her in that position. Maybe it was better he just wait until she was safely at the police station, write her a note explaining everything and disappear before they drew any closer.

"When are you going to stop running?" Zack's voice echoed in his mind. He grabbed for the air pump. He wasn't running. He was saving lives. He was changing the world. Doing all that just meant leaving some things behind.

There was the rumble of an engine coming from the direction of the parking lot. He glanced up. A black van had parked across the entrance of the parking lot. He pressed his back up against the wall and held his breath.

Four young men got out. Most were barely more than teenagers. Two had guns. They walked around the van like a ragtag army of petty criminals in search of a battle to fight. They were the kind of boys he'd seen in battlegrounds all over the world. Boys who fought just because someone told them to and didn't stop until they were too beaten down to move. One of them was Billy. Then Al stepped out. He glanced a cold eye over them like a guerrilla leader preparing for war.

Mark could feel the breath freeze inside of his lungs. For a second, he was almost paralyzed by the questions cascading through his brain. How had they found them? How could he fight? What if they ran?

Silent words tumbled over and over in his mind, pleading with God to do something—anything. He needed to make sure Katie was safe. He could not fail her. He needed to protect her even more than he needed to protect himself.

In that moment, something like a bolt of lightning shot through Mark's heart, splitting it down the middle and illuminating everything in its path. He needed help. He had one shot to get it. Nothing else mattered now.

ELEVEN

Hearing the vehicle pull up was what had first put Katie on edge. She'd been standing with her back to the fiberglass waterfall, idly swinging the putter back and forth, when she heard the guttural roar of a badly tuned engine shake the air. She tried to still her racing heart and tell herself it was probably nothing, even as she could feel her fingers clenching around the club in her hands. Then came the footsteps, moving slowly, as though someone was methodically searching for something.

Making herself as small as she could, she slid behind the final obstacle until she could look out in between the gap in the plastic trees. There were two of them—Billy and a larger boy. A long-barreled gun shook unsteadily in Billy's hands.

Terror poured through her limbs like an icy wave. If only she'd been able to find a better hiding place. She forced large deep breaths into her lungs. Billy stepped around the corner. His eyes scanned around the space and then fell on the corner where she crouched. His eyes met hers. He smirked. Then he raised the gun toward her face.

She swung. The sharp upswing of the golf club caught him across the temple, knocking the gun from his hands. Billy fell to his knees with a yelp. Katie didn't pause. Leaping out from behind the barrier, she came face-to-face with the other boy. He was taller and younger with the bloodshot eyes of someone who had already seen far more than a human being should and had made it through by brute force and dissociative drugs.

She held the putter out in front of her chest and tightened her grip. She might not be able to win, but there was nowhere to run now and at least she'd go down fighting. The boy snarled. A motor roared. He turned. The motorcycle shot out from behind the building. Through the helmet's open visor she could see Mark—his jaw set, face grim. Her helmet was clenched in his outstretched hand. He swung it around hard, catching her attacker in the chest and knocking him to the ground.

Mark swerved to a stop. "You okay?"

Katie ran to him. "Yeah. Billy's behind the waterfall. I hit him with a putter."

Mark grinned. "You are amazing."

He threw her the helmet. She caught it and shoved it on.

"There's at least two more boys, plus Al, and

they've got a van. They've blocked off the entrance to the parking lot, so get prepared to—"

A gunshot rang out in the air. Mark cried out in pain. He lurched sideways, nearly throwing himself and the bike sideways onto the ground. Katie grabbed for him and braced his weight to keep him from falling. Blood seeped through his sleeve, running down over his hand and onto the ground.

"Al! They're over here!"

She glanced back. Billy was crawling toward before them, gun waving in his hands. He pulled the trigger again. The bullet shot past them into the trees.

"Climb on," Mark said.

"You're shot!"

"I'm just grazed. I'll…" He groaned.

"Slide back. I'm driving."

"Can you?"

She threw her leg over the bike in front of him. "Better than you can. Just hold on."

Sweat was pouring down Mark's forehead. His face was ashen. Settling herself on the seat, she grabbed his good arm and threw it around her waist. He held on. There was shouting to her left and the sound of people running toward them. She didn't let herself look. Gritting her teeth, she yanked hard on the throttle. The bike shot forward. She hit the edge of the fourth hole and jumped onto the green, nearly taking out a fiberglass falcon before landing hard on the ground again. They flew down the verge and then out onto the road.

She'd driven motorbikes before but never something this large—and not with the weight of an injured body hanging on to her. *Help him, God... Help us, God... Help me...* She flew down the highway, forcing her arms to stay steady on the handlebars. She edged the bike faster, faster as rocks and trees flashed past her in a blur.

How far was it to the nearest town? How would she ever outrun them? Mark's grip was beginning to weaken. She could feel fear beginning to take root in her stomach and crawl up inside her. There was nothing but empty highway in front of them and an unknown, relentless enemy behind them. They would never escape. There was nowhere to run.

She heard the steady thrum of a new, heavier motor in the distance. Something else was coming now. Something big.

They were going to get captured. Kidnapped. Tied up like animals. And then?

She could hear the sound of the motor growing louder. Thrumming. Humming. Like it was floating through the air and about to land on top of them. She glanced in the rearview mirror. The van was still just a speck in the distance, growing larger by the second. But still the loud, disembodied sound of a motor droned on, drowning out even the sound of the engine beneath her.

They crested a hill, and then she saw it. A large black helicopter was coming down from the sky toward them. It hovered above the road, like a metallic beetle with dark tinted eyes, emblazoned with the logo of the Shields Corporation.

The door slid open. A rope ladder fell out. An imposing figure in a crisp black uniform climbed down and leaped onto the road in front of them. Another followed quickly on his heels. Mark's arm slipped from her waist. She pulled up on the accelerator, barely bringing the bike to a stop before he fell onto the ground. The men in uniform were pelting across the pavement toward them. Choking back tears, Katie jumped off and fell down to his side. She pulled Mark's helmet off and cradled his head onto her knees. "Trust me, Katie. Please..."

Strong hands clamped down on her shoulders, pulling her away from him.

The high-backed seats inside the helicopter were made of leather and melted around Katie's limbs like butter. The uniformed men who had escorted her there had practically forced her to sit. Then they went back down again on a stretcher, leaving her alone in the sleek, loungelike interior with the helicopter's one other passenger—a stunning, dark-haired woman in a flowing yellow dress and crisp black blazer.

"Are they going to get Mark? I'm not leaving without him."

The woman smirked. "I'm not sure you have much of a choice. But I can assure you we have no intention of leaving him behind." A polite smile spread across her face that didn't quite touch her eyes. It was the kind of faked smile intended to make you look warm while still holding yourself back. It took years of practice to make a smile like that look genuine. "I don't believe we've been introduced. I'm Sunny Shields, chief of operations for Shields Corp. You can call me Sunny."

Katie couldn't even begin to guess why the CEO of the Shields Corporation would airlift her off the highway. But at least no one was firing at them.

"I'm Katie Todd with *Impact News*. I was invited up here to cover the events this weekend. My friend Mark runs a small charity."

Sunny's eyebrows rose. Okay, whatever she was expecting her to say, it was definitely not that. But all Sunny said in reply was, "You're going to want to buckle your seat belt."

The black-clad figures reappeared in the doorway with Mark strapped to the stretcher. His eyes were shut, but thankfully his chest was still moving. Had he passed out, or had they sedated him? The men nodded to Sunny. Then they carried him to the back portion of the cavernous aircraft and pulled a door shut behind them. Katie followed them with her eyes.

Now what? Fighting off a teenager with a gun was one thing but trying to safely bring down an aircraft full of armed guards was something else entirely—especially if Mark was on board and injured.

"How was he hurt?" Sunny asked. Was there a glimmer of genuine concern slipping through her clipped tones?

"He was grazed in the arm by a bullet. We need to get him to a hospital."

Sunny waved a hand toward a closed-circuit camera. The helicopter rose. "All of my security team have medical training. If they think we need to land at a hospital or clinic, they'll let me know." Sunny moved her eyes toward the window. "I'm afraid you're just going to have to trust me."

"Trust you? Are you kidding me? Since agreeing to cover your father's party I've been attacked, kidnapped, tied up and shot at. Not to mention crashing a truck and jumping from a moving vehicle."

Sunny's eyes swiveled forward. The calm mask fell from her face to show the pure shock underneath. Beautifully manicured fingers rose to her throat. "Kidnapped?"

"Yes. Kidnapped. And while I may not have a clue how to safely land a helicopter, I'd sooner try that right now than just trust anyone from the almighty Shields Corporation—"

"I can assure you that nobody from Shields had anything to do with any of—"

"Why is someone trying to kidnap me?"

"I don't know—"

"Does the name Langtry Glen mean anything to you?" Katie asked.

She was hoping for a big response, but all Sunny did was sniff. "Of course. It's a property we acquired four years ago. Why?"

"Because…" How much could she trust her? Probably not all that much. "Because maybe somebody who lived there still holds a grudge."

This time Sunny rolled her eyes. "You can't be serious. We've received some threats from people who weren't happy with the acquisition, but that was years ago and our security consultants assured us it was nothing to worry about."

"Look, I know how ridiculous this must sound. But I can assure you that whoever's been chasing me means business."

Sunny crossed her arms over her chest. Her eyes narrowed. "What makes you so sure someone's after you?"

Had she not just noticed the men with guns or seen that Mark was injured? The helicopter soared over the treetops as a constant kaleidoscope of pictures flashed through Katie's mind.

"Because someone is. I was followed up on the

train from Toronto, and they jumped me in the station parking lot. If Mark hadn't been there, I'd probably be dead by now. One of my kidnappers had a Langtry Glen bandanna, presumably to set them up. For all I know, it was someone inside your own organization. Maybe it was even you, and that's why your security grabbed us—"

"They saved you!"

"Why would they do that? For that matter, why would you come with them?"

A dangerous look flashed across Sunny's dark eyes. She opened her mouth. Her hand raised in the air as if to strike a chord. Then she paused, chuckled under her breath and lowered her hand again. She crossed her arms. "Mark asked for help, and he's never asked me for anything before. Ever." Her voice was calm with the threat of some deep-seated emotion moving beneath the surface. "Until now. Until you." Her glance swept critically from the top of Katie's disheveled hair all the way down over the borrowed clothes to her mud-caked shoes. "I guess you could say I was curious."

Katie's heart stopped. "You know Mark?"

"I used to think I did. But considering the fact you obviously know nothing about what's happening here. I suggest you stop talking before you embarrass yourself."

"But—"

"When you do find out what Mark's deal is, you're definitely not going to hear it from me." It was the tone of a woman who was used to being listened to.

The helicopter started descending. They flew over a golf course, set on the edge of a river-fed lake, with a lushly forested island near the center. Then a set of walls with a guarded gate and then a ring of four buildings around a large green space.

"This is the Shields Corporation headquarters?"

At least Sunny should be willing to answer that question.

"It is. When my father was younger, he liked the idea of living at work for some reason. Made it easier for him to just work through life, I presume. The two biggest buildings used to be Shields Corp offices. The medium-sized one was the family home, and the smallest was a row of townhouse apartments for guests."

"Why are you talking like this was all in the past?"

"As you'll no doubt discover at the media brunch tomorrow," Sunny said drily, "my father has been making some changes."

Gently, the helicopter flew over the buildings before dropping down on a small, square helipad. Sunny had her seat belt off before they had even touched ground. The door to the helicopter opened. A young blond man in an expensive suit reached for Sunny's hand. But she stepped back and waved Katie on ahead of her.

"Hurry," Sunny said. "We need to get Mark to a doctor."

Katie let the blond man take her hand and help her down the stairs and out from under the propeller blades. Then she turned back toward Sunny. But to her horror, the helicopter door was beginning to close.

"Wait!" she shouted.

The helicopter rose in the air again, and it disappeared into the setting sun. Taking Mark's unconscious body with it. Leaving her behind.

TWELVE

"Ms. Todd?" said a voice at her elbow. "I'm Tim Albright."

Jonah Shields's personal secretary had broad shoulders and closely cropped hair. He smiled politely and extended a hand to shake hers.

"You can call me Katie. Where are they taking him?"

"My understanding is that they are taking him to a doctor."

"Where?"

"The nearest clinic is in Kapuskasing, but Ms. Shields thought you'd be more comfortable waiting here."

Of course she did.

"I understand some unfortunate circumstances prevented you from attending this afternoon's briefing," he added. "So I've taken the liberty of putting together a folder for you with some information about the company and its history."

She nearly laughed. Was she just supposed to

go ahead with the story now as if none of this had happened?

"You'll find it in your rooms," he went on. "Also, we were informed by the Cobalt police that your luggage was stolen. So when I heard from Ms. Shields that you were arriving, I took the liberty of having someone lay out a few things. Now, if you'll be so kind to follow me."

She didn't move. "What do you mean my rooms?"

"It was felt by Mr. Shields that you would be more comfortable staying with us on site."

"Are any of the other media staying here?"

He shifted from one foot to the other. "No."

"Then why me? Seriously? What's going on here? I mean, I just got airlifted off the highway in a helicopter."

His back straightened. "I'm afraid you'll have to ask Mr. Shields that. Now, if you'd be so kind as to follow me."

Katie pressed her lips together. She glanced up to where the last dying streaks of red and gold were brushing the indigo wash of evening sky. The sun had set, leaving her no closer to answers.

But as long as she was just standing here on a helipad, her options were pretty limited. She followed him through the complex toward a small row of townhouses. The grounds were tidy, but the buildings were more modest than she'd expected.

He opened the door for the second townhouse and handed her the key.

"I've already taken the liberty of informing the police of your whereabouts." He pulled a card from his pocket and handed it to her. "But of course, I presume you'd like to talk to them yourself. Just call this number and ask for Officer Ward."

"Thank you, and how about my friend?"

"I will let you know if I hear anything."

He closed the door behind him. She let out a long sigh and locked the door. *Okay, Lord, now what?* There was a spacious living room with dark leather furniture. French doors led out to a balcony, overlooking the same green lawn she'd seen from the helicopter. Someone had laid an array of sandwiches, pastries and fruit out on the counter of the kitchenette. In a bright yellow master bedroom, she found several outfits laid out on the bed—skirts, shorts, tops, dresses, sandals, along with toiletries and makeup. Everything she needed except, of course, answers.

She forced herself to eat, then washed and changed into simple yoga pants and a jersey top as quickly as she could—trying not to let herself obsess about where Mark was. Then she called the Cobalt police station, thankful to hear both Officers Sakes and Parks were on duty. After assurance that the name and number Albright had given her was genuine, she called the Kapuskasing station and filed another report with Officer Ward, making sure to mention that one of the kidnappers had a bandanna from Langtry Glen.

Finally, she called her boss. Ethan answered on the first ring. "Where on earth are you? Why haven't you been filing any stories? You better still be on track to cover the Shields thing."

A tight smile crossed her lips. "Actually, I'm in the Shields complex right now."

He let out a loud, unflattering cross between a snort and a gasp. "At this hour? I thought you'd be in your hotel by now." That seemed to knock him back one. Not that he was the type to admit it.

"Actually, they've arranged guest rooms for me."

"Not without clearing it by me first."

"Are you kidding? I thought you'd be dying for an inside scoop."

There was a long pause on the other end of the line. "Well. Okay. But I'm expecting regular updates from you from now on. You got that? This story is too important for us to lose over some mishap."

"Mishap? Like being kidnapped?" She lay down on the couch and leaned her head back on one of the arms. "For that matter, since when do parties at a rich guy's house qualify as important? There's a bigger story here somewhere, isn't there? That's why you sent me up here so suddenly. You got some tip from one of your clubbing buddies that something big was going down? The old man getting married again to someone young and unsuitable? His wayward son planning a takeover? Something involving someone you know? A friend? A family member? Someone on the board? Look, if there's something I need to know to do my job—"

"This conversation is pointless." Ethan sniffed. "You know your job, Katie. I expect you to go do it." Then the phone went dead.

Wow. Katie tucked the phone beside her on the couch and lay back. She closed her eyes and started mapping out the facts of the past few days in her mind like she would a news story waiting to be written. A rich man was holding a party. Strangers had made several, increasingly violent and risky attempts to kidnap her. Her belongings had been stolen. A Shields helicopter had descended unexpectedly from the sky, taking Mark's unconscious body away with them.

Then there was Mark. The strength in his arms. The feel of his hand on the small of her back as she'd nestled into his arms. The warmth of his lips as they'd brushed along her hairline.

She yanked an afghan off the back of the couch and wrapped it around herself as an ache spread inside her chest. Despite everything she didn't know— the questions, the doubts, the random facts piling up that made no sense no matter how she turned them around in her mind—one thing was clear. She missed him. Missed his smile, his laugh. Most of all, she missed that sense of peace and security that had come from knowing he was there beside her. Here was a man she could admire. A man worthy of respect. Who had risked his life to protect hers. Who might even have been about to kiss her at the gas station if she hadn't pushed him back. And now he was hurt and gone, and she wasn't sure when she'd see him again. She blinked back tears that suddenly rushed to her eyes.

Please, God. Please let him be okay...

The memory of Mark's face filled her mind. The strength in his jaw, the tenderness in his mouth, the depth of concern in his eyes. *"Trust me, Katie. Please..."* His voice drifted through her thoughts as she slipped into a fitful sleep.

Mark steadied his hand on the door frame. The morning sun was creeping over the horizon. His stomach was in knots. He'd barely slept, let alone had much of a stomach for breakfast. Of all the doors he'd knocked on in his life, he couldn't remember ever being this worried about what would greet him on the other side. He took a deep breath and knocked twice. The door swung back. Then Mark saw Katie.

Her hair was fringed with golden hues, backlit by rays of sun filtering through the windows. A relieved sob escaped from her lips. "I didn't know what had happened to you." Tears shone in the corners of her eyes. "Or if I was ever going to see you again."

"I'm so sorry." He pulled her into his arms and buried his face in her hair. His mouth brushed over her trembling eyelids and down across her cheeks until finally touching ever so lightly on her lips. Then he pulled back and rested his forehead against hers, feeling her breath against his face. "I tried to get to you sooner. I needed a couple of stitches, and they insisted on holding me overnight in case I had a concussion. Then it took some time to find you."

She ran her fingers down his arm. "You're okay, though?"

He nodded and pushed up his sleeve and showed her the small white bandage. "Honestly, it was nothing. They would have discharged me right away if they hadn't been concerned I hit my head." He followed her into the living room. "How are you?"

"I'm okay." She squeezed his hand. "I was mostly worried for you. Not to mention confused—"

"Mr. Shields!" Albright appeared in the doorway, holding both a coffee tray and attaché case. "What an unexpected surprise."

"It's Mark, please." Instinct kicked in before he could even process what had happened.

Katie let go of his hand. Her hand rose to her lips. For a moment, Mark thought she was going to scream. Then his heart twisted in his chest as he watched instead as an eerie, emotionless calm spread across her features.

"Mr. Shields would be pleased if you would both meet him for coffee at your earliest convenience." Albright set a tray down on the counter. He smiled at Katie. "Mr. Shields is especially looking forward to meeting you. While he is extending this morning's invitation as a purely social visit, he is also happy to arrange a private interview on the record later this afternoon after the press conference.

"I took the liberty of finding you a computer to assist you in your coverage of today's events." He pulled a slim laptop from the case and set it down beside the coffee. "There are some gowns hanging in the closet to choose from for this evening. However, if you would like to go shopping for something more suitable, we can arrange for a car to take you to the nearest town."

Katie nodded. Her lips unfroze long enough to thank him and smile. But Mark noticed the smile came nowhere near reaching her eyes. What must she be thinking?

"I presume you'll be needing a suitable wardrobe for today's events, as well, sir?" Albright turned to Mark. "May I suggest a suit for the morning and a tuxedo for this evening?"

Mark swallowed hard. "Please thank my father for his hospitality, but I'm afraid I'm not planning on staying for the day. I will be in touch later about rescheduling my meeting."

Albright nodded.

"Do you happen to know what happened to the motorcycle I was riding yesterday? I'm afraid it didn't come with me in the helicopter, and I must return it to a friend."

"A van was sent to collect it. I believe there was some question as to whether it had been damaged, so it was taken to a garage in Kapuskasing. I will inquire. If either of you require a car, I'd be happy to arrange one. If there's anything else I can assist with, please don't hesitate to call."

"Thank you."

Albright stepped out, closing the door behind him.

Mark turned toward Katie. "I'm sorry. I can explain..."

"Jonah Shields is your father?" The words were calm. Her voice level.

He nodded slowly.

"You're Jonah Shields Junior..." Again, her tone was so composed. Like a consummate reporter, just checking the facts, making sure she had the story straight.

"I was. But I haven't been my father's son for years..."

"You *lied* to me."

"No, I didn't. In fact, I was very careful not to. We never really discussed our families or our pasts—"

"Don't you dare give me that lame excuse!" The composure dropped in an instant as a flash of irritation swept across her face. "We didn't discuss a lot of things, but that didn't stop you from kissing me just a few moments ago. I'll accept that you never actually lied to me. But you sure didn't tell me the entire truth, either."

"Yes, I did. I told you the only truth about me that matters. None of this—" he turned to the window and swung his arm out toward the buildings of the Shields Corporation "—has anything to do with me. Yes, I grew up in the shadow of these buildings, but they don't define who I am. I'm an engineer. I founded a small charity and run around the world finding ways to make people's lives better. I walked away from my family empty-handed. Nothing but the clothes on my back and the key to the safety deposit box my grandmother left me. I am not Jonah Shields Junior anymore. I haven't been in a long time."

Her arms crossed in front of her chest. "Is your name even Mark?"

He fought the urge to sigh. Was she going to question everything now? Yeah, he probably deserved that. "Yes. My legal name is now Mark Armor. My middle name was Mark, and that's what my family and friends always called me growing up. Armor was my grandmother's maiden name. I changed my name legally the day I turned nineteen."

Katie rolled her shoulders slowly. She walked over to the patio doors and then back toward the couch as though she were trapped in some kind of puzzle and trying to find her way out again.

"People treat me differently when they find out who my father is. Like I somehow have access to my family's wealth or some kind of say in Shields Corp business decisions. Is it so wrong that I wanted for you to get to know me for me?"

"Yes." She neatly spun on the balls of her feet. "Yes, it is, Mark. Because it's not like we just started chatting at a party. You knew my life was in danger. You knew I was headed here. And you decided it was more important to protect yourself than take care of me—"

He stiffened. "That's not fair. Everything I did was about trying to protect you."

"Are you sure? Or were you just trying to avoid conflict? Waiting until the last possible minute to tell me so that you wouldn't have to deal with the fallout of answering questions you didn't want to answer?" She groaned. "So this is what you and Zack were arguing about..."

"He worked for my family when I was a teenager."

"Which is why he knew about the GPS," she gasped. "That's why the Shields helicopter swept out of the sky and rescued us. You set off the emergency beacon!"

"Yes. I did. I saw Al and his crew pull up, and I knew I wasn't that far from my family, so I figured this was my best chance of getting help. But I didn't know if anyone was still monitoring the signal. I didn't even know my sister had come along for the helicopter ride until someone at the hospital told me. I haven't seen her in years."

"Do you have any idea how frightened I was?" she demanded, fighting the urge to scream. "I had no clue whether or not I could trust these people or where they were taking you. For all I knew, they were kidnapping both of us. What if I'd done something reckless, like try to escape? What if your need to keep secrets put me in even greater danger?"

He crossed his arms in front of his chest. Now she was being ridiculous. "I said I was sorry. But I did what I thought was right. What if you had decided you hated my father so much you wouldn't let me help you?"

"Then it was my choice to make." Fire flashed in her eyes. "You asked me to trust you, but you hardly trusted me. You should've told me before we'd even left the farmhouse." She ran her hands up through her hair and clenched it at the roots for a moment before letting it fall through her fingers again. "Or were you afraid I'd call up my boss and say, 'Hey, new scoop. Jonah Shields's son is running a near-bankrupt charity'?"

He turned toward the window.

She took in a sharp breath. "Wow. You actually thought I might. That's how little you trusted me."

"If this gets reported in the media, it will kill TRUST." His shoulders sagged. "We'll be blacklisted. Our funding will dry up. No one will be willing to let the son of the almighty, evil Jonah Shields so much as change a lightbulb."

"So it's not just me." She sighed softly. "You don't actually trust anyone."

He turned back. Her arms had dropped to her side, and the anger in her eyes was replaced by a much softer look than he'd ever expected to see there again.

"Let me guess," she said. "You dash into a problem, solve it and run away again before anyone has a chance to take care of you in return?" Her voice was gentle. Probably a lot gentler than he deserved under the circumstances.

But even so, he could feel the muscles in his jaw tightening and that old familiar tension spreading across his shoulders. "You don't understand."

"Yes, I actually do. The women in my family have a habit of marrying untrustworthy men who hurt them. My boss would let me spin the wind if it suited his whim. I know what it's like to be afraid of trusting anyone. Believe me, I do. People can be pretty irrational and self-serving, and a lot of them aren't worth putting your faith in. But I'm not like that. You should have given me a shot with the truth.

I deserved that much. And as long as you're going through life trying to hide away such a big part of yourself, you're not giving anyone a chance. Not a chance to care about you. Not a chance to surprise you. Not a chance for them to understand you. Because you're too busy trying to control how much of you they're even allowed to love."

Her voice was gentle, but still something about the comment stuck under his skin like a thorn. None of this had anything to do with love. It was about responsibility. It was about doing what needed to be done.

He ran his hand over the back of his neck. But he'd been foolish. He'd let himself care about her in a way he had no right caring about anyone, and in the process, he had led her on. Now her feelings were hurt. Well, he had delivered her safely to where she needed to be. Now it was time to move on.

"I'm sorry for hurting you, but I did what I thought was best." He walked to the sliding glass doors and slid them open. "I apologize for kissing you. That was foolish. I think it's best I leave now before the media circus begins. If you want to get in touch, you can send me a message via Nick. Just know it may be weeks before I'm able to respond. I'm actually leaving the country the day after tomorrow and will be gone for months."

He stepped out onto the balcony and scanned the courtyard below. A spiral staircase led down to the courtyard to where a large, white marquee tent was spread across the lawn. The space was deserted now, except for a lone gardener in a battered cowboy hat who was clipping the last of the dead flowers off the bushes. A pickup truck was parked nearby. Could he risk asking the man for a ride out of the complex? "I'd better get out of here before anyone else recognizes me. The last thing I want is for the projects we're helping to suffer because other people can't handle where I come from."

She crossed the room in three steps. Her hand slid onto his arm. "Are you sure it's other people who can't handle where you come from?"

He gripped the railing with both hands. "I've got to go. I'm going to hitchhike to Kapuskasing. If anyone asks, you can just tell them I walked off."

"Well, then I guess this is goodbye." She let go of his arm and stepped back. "Thank you for everything."

He shut his eyes tightly. He couldn't risk looking back. "Stay safe."

"You, too."

He sprinted down the staircase.

She clenched her fists so tightly her nails pressed into her palms and watched as he ran across the lawn. He didn't even notice the gardener tilt up the brim of his hat and call out to him as he passed.

How *dare* he? Yes, his family history was messy

and complex. And she could hardly blame him for not wanting to stick around for a day's worth of events. But that didn't justify hiding the truth from her. Or running away.

Was she ever going to see him again?

No, she couldn't let herself think about that right now. She was still here to do a job—like it or not. She needed to be professional. She walked back into the living room and opened the laptop. It connected to the internet immediately. Idly, she opened her email. The first message was from her editor.

Katie
Breaking news. Big scoop. I expect you to get on this immediately.
Ethan

She clicked the attachment. Her heart stopped in her chest as a grainy picture of Mark loading his truck outside Celia's farmhouse filled the screen, under this headline: *Busted. Son of Real Estate Mogul, Jonah Junior, Runs Secret Charity.*

His identity had been blown wide-open and in the worst possible way. Almost every gossip news site had the story and photo—including *Impact News*.

How had this happened? Well, she could guess. Billy had taken their pictures at the farmhouse. Then, sometime after ambushing them on the road, they'd gone through Mark's belongings and realized who he was. He was sure to carry a government-issued ID with both his old and new name on it. But to sell that information to the tabloids? Why? Were her kidnappers media-savvy opportunists? Or was there something more insidious in play?

One thing was clear. Whoever had been after her knew who he was. They probably also knew where to find him. She slammed the laptop closed. She needed to warn him that his identity had been blown, especially if there was even a chance that it put his life in danger.

She ran down the stairs into the courtyard and sprinted across the lawn toward the elderly gardener. "Hey! I need your help!"

He stood slowly, wiping his hands on dirty, tattered jeans. She caught a glimpse of a wrinkled, sun-scorched face framed by a trim white beard.

"My friend just came through here." She gasped for breath. "He was walking to the highway. Did you see where he went?"

"Is everything all right?" Fierce blue eyes looked into hers.

"No. I need to catch up with him. It's important. Please. Can you help me?"

He nodded. "We'll take my truck. He'll have taken the main road. It won't take long to catch up with him."

"Thank you."

* * *

The pickup was large and the color of dying embers, with the kind of wide base that implied it was used to carrying heavy loads. They drove through the main gates and out onto a rural road. Moments later, they reached the highway. The gardener paused for a moment. "He's heading toward Kapuskasing?"

"Yup."

He turned left.

"Do you live in the complex?" she asked.

"I used to. Now I live in a cottage I built, just outside it. It's very simple and quite small. But it's all I really need."

They crested a hill, and she could see the unmistakable outline of Mark in the distance. *Thank you, God.* "That's him."

A low, black car pulled to a stop beside him. Mark exchanged a few words with the driver. Then he climbed in the passenger door. The gardener honked his horn and flashed his lights. Katie waved out the window. The car took off. She sighed. *Now what?*

"Don't worry." The gardener accelerated. "There's an intersection about fifteen minutes away. I'll pull up beside him then."

"Thanks. I'm just really sorry to take you away from your work."

His smile was dry. "Oh, the gardening? It's really just a hobby—"

His voice was lost in the blare of a car horn and

the screeching of wheels. The car ahead of them swerved hard, weaving back and forth. Mark must have been fighting the driver for control of the wheel. A gunshot split the air. The car's passenger window exploded in a cascade of glass.

THIRTEEN

The car straightened and sped away.

Color drained from the gardener's face. "He's in trouble."

"Yeah. It's—"

"Hang on. I'm going to force them over." He gunned the engine.

Within minutes, the larger, stronger vehicle had caught up with the smaller one and pulled alongside it. She started to roll down the window and then stopped. The young man driving was the same one who had threatened her at the mini-golf course. She couldn't even see Mark.

The truck edged ahead of the car. They pulled in front of it, blocked its path and then began to gradually slow. Any luck and they could just carefully slow down until the car was forced to stop.

But instead, the car turned sharply, trying to U-turn around them. The driver lost control. The car flew off the road. It hit the ditch and rolled twice before landing upside down. The gardener hit the brakes and grabbed his phone. Katie leaped out and ran toward the wreck.

Mark was crawling out the shattered passenger window.

"You okay?"

"Yeah. Thanks to you. This guy offered me a ride and then pulled a gun on me. I tried to force him over. But then he shot out my window. Last thing I wanted was for him to try to keep shooting in a speeding car." He straightened slowly, brushing off broken glass. "How did you know I was in trouble?"

"I didn't. Your picture is all over the internet. It looks like whoever wanted to kidnap me used the information they stole to expose you online. But I don't know why—"

The teenager crawled out of the car, a gun shaking unsteadily in his hand. But before they could react, there was the metallic sound of a shotgun cocking behind them.

"Drop the gun, and keep your hands where we can see them." It was a voice of authority. She turned. There was a pump action shotgun in the gardener's steady hands. "You okay, son?" The cowboy hat had slipped down his back. For the first time, she looked past the well-worn jeans and mud-stained boots and straight into the fierce, weathered face of the man she'd met in the garden. Her hand rose to her chest.

It was Jonah Shields.

* * *

The porch swing creaked gently. Mark looked out over the lush small garden that spilled out behind his father's simple log cabin. His. Father's. Log. Cabin. Now there were four words he never expected to go together. He risked a glance at the woman sitting beside him. He knew he should say something. But words failed him. For the moment, he was just thankful she was there.

"Last time I saw my father he was living in a six-bedroom house." It almost felt like an odd thing to comment on, considering the plethora of police and Shields's staff currently swarming the cabin behind them. His father's house was so full of uniforms; it was standing room only. Local police had even invited officers from Cobalt to consult.

Both cops and Shields's security had arrived in droves within minutes of the car flipping, which probably meant his father had called them from the truck. Yeah, his father now drove a pickup. Add that to everything else going on that required answers.

True, he had long stopped listening to his father's voice messages. But he'd expected them to still be filled with the reminder that he was disappointed and angry—not the news he was firing his chauffeur, moving out of the Shields complex and dramatically rearranging his priorities.

"He told me he built his place," Katie said.

"Well, he did get his start building houses." Not

that he'd ever expected his dad to pick up a hammer again.

Katie leaned her head on Mark's shoulder and, while he guessed it was more out of exhaustion than anything else, there was something about the simple gesture that sent waves of relief coursing through him. When security had escorted them to his father's cottage, he'd half expected her to still be frustrated with him. And maybe she was. But when he'd suggested they pop outside for a chance to talk in private, she'd just slipped onto the porch swing beside him and waited for him to start—for which he was grateful.

The back of her hand brushed against his. "We need answers," she said, "and I'm tired of not getting them."

"Me, too."

"I didn't know that was your dad, by the way. He was just tending the bushes, and I asked him to help me catch up to you."

He'd run by his father without even noticing him. "So now, the whole world knows that Mark Armor, charity engineer, started his life as Jonah Shields Junior."

"Just those who read gossip."

He smiled slightly, despite himself. "But that still doesn't explain why I can't get two steps outside Shields Corp without having a total stranger pull a gun on me. Don't get me wrong. Being recognized as my father's son is never all that easy. But it's awkward—not deadly. Not to mention that we still don't know why someone was after you." He glanced back toward the cabin. "They'll probably be ratcheting up tonight's security so high you'll practically need a retina scan to reach the punch bowl. You said you'd seen the guy who tried kidnapping me before?"

"At the gas station yesterday," she said. "You hit him with the helmet. I know Billy had a Langtry Glen bandanna, but I just can't imagine any of the residents holding enough of a grudge that they'd chase me across northern Ontario. But if this whole thing was just about someone trying to crash today's event, does that mean by tomorrow it's all going to be over, and we can both go back to life as usual?"

Whatever *usual* was going to look like now.

"I wish I knew." He glanced up at the sky and pictured his workshop. It would be so much easier if he could just tackle this like a piece of broken equipment. Lay it all out on the table, take it apart, examine and test each component until he'd isolated what had gone wrong and why. The trick was to start by ruling out possibilities and work backward from there.

"Okay, let's begin with what we already know," he said. "We know they targeted you before you'd even met me."

"But it's still got to be linked to this assignment somehow," she said. "Otherwise, why hadn't anyone tried to kidnap me before I took the train here? Besides, there's nothing valuable or special about me—"

"No, you're amazing." He leaned the top of his head against hers for a moment and just breathed her in. "And I'm glad that you're here with me."

There was a sudden outburst of shouting from inside the cabin. The door flew open, and his sister stormed out. Sunny was dressed to kill in a slick white business suit and string of black pearls. Her steel-gray stilettos clacked on the wood. Her eyes flashed.

"Did you know that you've got a fifty thousand dollar bounty on your head?"

"What?" he said. "No!"

Sunny's lids narrowed. "Not you." She pointed a long, French-tipped finger at Katie. "Her!"

Mark leaped off the porch swing. Sunny stepped into her big brother's chest.

"What's going on here?" she demanded. "I don't see you in three years, and then suddenly you show up, out of the blue, with a wanted woman who every two-bit criminal in miles is likely to be chasing after. Do you even know who she is or what kind of game she's running?"

"I am exactly who I say I am." Katie rose to her feet. "I was invited up here by your company to cover this weekend's events—which I'm sure you already know."

"This is between me and my brother. I'll thank you to stay out of it."

"No." Katie's arms crossed in front of her chest. "With all due respect, it isn't. I realize there's a lot going on right now, and you're probably really stressed. But my life is in danger, and trying to sideline me isn't going to help anybody."

Mark felt a surge of pride. Sunny's mouth gaped. For a second, her hand raised as if to…what? Fire her? Suspend her? Have her removed from the premises? If the whole thing wasn't so deadly serious, he'd have almost been tempted to laugh. He couldn't imagine people tried standing up to his sister all that often. But Sunny just sucked in a hard breath, turned on her heels and marched back into the cottage.

Mark's arm slid around Katie's shoulder. "Chances are you're the first person to shut her down in years."

She glanced at him sideways. "Just don't you start sidelining me again, either."

The door swung open again, and three cops walked out: Officers Parks and Sakes, who'd been brought up from Cobalt, as well as the shaggy-haired Kapuskasing veteran, who was Officer Ward. Detective Brant, who'd come up all the way from Sudbury that morning to lead the investigation, followed them. The tall woman with long red hair and determined features had the build of an Olympic athlete and a clear, no-nonsense way of asking questions.

At least no one could say the police weren't taking it seriously.

Mark turned to Brant. "Is it true? Has someone actually put a price on Katie's head?"

"Yes, it appears so." She turned to Katie. "I do apologize for not informing you through the proper channels. It appears Ms. Shields overheard two officers talking and did not realize that we were in the process of confirming the information."

That was a polite way of putting it, Mark thought.

Brant walked over to the patio set and gestured for them to sit. Then she sat down across from them and set her arms on the table. "The driver of the car is a young man from North Bay named Carl Lane. He's seventeen years old and is known to local police. Heavy drug use mostly. Some crime—assaults, breaking and entering—to support his drug habit. But he is not someone who police had reason to believe would be involved in something of this nature."

"Does he have anything to do with Langtry Glen?" Katie asked.

"No. As far as we can tell, he's never even been to Toronto. He does, however, frequent some particularly nasty websites dedicated to sharing information on how to illegally modify weapons and build homemade explosives. We do have a task force monitoring many of these sites for signs of potential illegal activity, but of course new ones spring up all the time."

"How does any of this relate back to Katie?"

"He's claiming that yesterday morning someone posted a notice on one of these sites looking for people to help with kidnapping her."

"You must be joking." For a moment, Mark had to clench his hands together to keep from banging them on the table. "You're telling me that this kid threatened our lives yesterday and today just because of something someone wrote on a website?"

Brant nodded. "The notice has now been removed from the site, but we were able to confirm its existence. It stated there was a fifty thousand dollar reward for kidnapping 'Katie Todd of *Impact News*' and that everyone who helped would get a cut. There was a photo, too, in case anyone was lucky enough to catch her solo. It appears to have been taken at the guesthouse where you both stayed in Cobalt."

Which could explain why Billy had been taking pictures at Celia's. Had Al put the photo together with the identification in Mark's stolen wallet and realized he could make some side money in a tabloid deal?

"For an unemployed kid with a taste for both drugs and violence, it must have looked like a really easy way to make some fast money," Brant went on. "He called a cell phone number—which has now been disconnected—and was told where to meet the posse and to bring his own weapon. It appears he failed to get the names of anyone he met, and most of them were wearing bandannas."

Mark ran his hand over his head. If it wasn't so serious, it would almost be laughable.

"He had a Langtry Glen bandanna in the glove compartment of his car," she said, "which he said a man named Al gave him in case he wanted to disguise his face. He just figured that Ms. Todd had upset an old boyfriend who was looking to get back at her."

Katie shrugged. "I've already given the police a complete personal history. I've been on a handful of first dates since moving to Toronto. But none in months and certainly none with anyone I imagine would come after me. To be honest, I'm more concerned about how this is connected to a story I covered years ago."

Mark squeezed her hand. "You said that someone had been dealing drugs in the building."

"Yes, and they never caught him. I realize that when Shields Corp demolished the community that at least one drug dealer lost the base of his criminal enterprise. Between the steady stream of vulnerable people coming to the drop-in program and the underemployed relying on government assistance, the place must have looked like easy pickings. He could have easily swiped a box of Langtry Glen bandannas when the buildings were destroyed. And he'd have reason to want revenge on the Shieldses. But that still doesn't explain why he'd target me or set such a big price on my head. Do we even know why this kid went after Mark this morning?"

"That was apparently all his idea," the detective said, drily. "Carl noticed you were picked up by a Shields helicopter so figured he'd just stake out the local roads and hope he got lucky. He apparently drove around the back road for hours." She turned to Mark. "It appears he had no reason for grabbing you other than the hope that he could lead you to her. Although he does remember hearing Al saying something yesterday about taking you both alive."

"What was he going to with Katie when he got her?"

"He hadn't gotten that far yet. Said he figured he'd call the number and demand the whole amount. Hadn't even crossed his mind that the number might not still be in order or that whoever posted the ad might not even have that amount of money, let alone be willing to pay him. He's not the brightest spark."

Mark rubbed his fingers against his temples. Sunny's analysis hadn't been that far off—someone had hung a Wanted sign around Katie's neck, and now she was prey to every stupid criminal with internet access. "I'm afraid there's more. The investigation into the rockslide on the train tracks north of Cobalt has determined it wasn't an accident."

Katie sucked in a breath. "What happened?"

The detective's expression was as still as stone.

"Explosives. Crude ones. Someone intentionally sent those rocks falling onto the train tracks."

Katie's face paled. Brant reached for her arm.

"But we still don't know if there's any connection between someone taking out the train tracks and your attempted kidnapping." The detective's voice was kind. "There are dozens of places that someone could have made an attempt to kidnap you without resorting to something so drastic. Why not wait until you reached Kapuskasing? Or try why you were still in Toronto? Why Cobalt?"

Why indeed. Mark's arms crossed tightly. His fists clenched. "You can't just expect us to sit here and accept that Katie's life is in danger from some unknown criminal, for some unknown reason, and there's nothing we can do about it—while he's out there amassing a ragtag bunch of petty criminals to help him."

Brant smiled grimly. "There is plenty that we can do and are doing. We have a forensic team examining the explosives. We are working with internet providers to trace the source of the original internet post looking for amateur kidnappers and monitor any similar ones that may appear. We've already spoken to several news sources about the online gossip that appeared about you this morning, looking for a possible connection, and we've learned they were all sent an identical email from a dummy email address. We are trying to determine if anyone formally associated with Langtry Glen has a criminal history. We are also working with Shields's staff here on security for today's events, which I believe are to begin shortly."

Mark glanced down at his watch. It was almost eleven. He'd figured he'd be long gone by now. Now here he was, stuck in his father's home, reluctant to leave Katie's side again. He turned to Katie. "It's about time I go talk to my father."

The warm, wood-beamed living room was empty now except for Sunny, who was curled in an overstuffed chair behind the fireplace. It was the same chair that had once sat in his grandmother's sunroom. Her feet were tucked up beside her. Whatever she was reading on her phone was making her smile.

Hard to believe he and his sister had been friends once—or at least joint allies in the craziness of the Shields world. What had happened to them? She'd always been headstrong, stubborn, smart and brave. He hadn't just loved his little sister; he'd admired her.

"Where did everybody go?" he asked.

She didn't even look up. "There are two private security guards and two police manning the driveway to this place. Dad is in his room getting changed. The rest have gone back to prepare for his brunch thing."

"Why aren't you there?"

"Did you not just hear what I said? This event is all our father's idea. I've had absolutely nothing to do with it."

"Really?"

She shot him a dirty look. "Is that what you think? That since you left I've been running around here throwing parties? I haven't had a single day off since you walked out of here and everything fell onto me. The responsibilities, the stress, the headaches—it's all been on my shoulders. Not to mention the endless, worried calls from stakeholders wondering why on earth Shields Corp has suddenly put the brakes on." She glanced at Katie. "Since my brother seems intent on keeping you around, let me make one thing perfectly clear. You are here as a personal guest of my family and not as a reporter. Consider everything you hear outside of today's official events as one hundred percent off the record, and if I catch one whiff of you reporting even a single word of my family's private business, I will sue you for breach of confidence. Is that clear?"

Katie nodded. "Got it."

Sunny looked back to her phone.

"Hang on," Mark said. "What has Father been—"

A door behind him closed. They turned. Jonah had walked in behind him. Gone now were the muddy work clothes, replaced instead with a steel-gray suit and navy tie, which made him look every bit the man and leader that he was.

"I'm glad you're here." He gestured at Mark and Katie to sit. Then he sat down in an armchair across from his daughter. "I had been hoping to talk to you both before the guests arrived. As I'll be outlining in more detail shortly, I've been doing some major restructuring of Shields Corp—"

Sunny snorted. "Cancelled projects, sold properties, paid off debts and gotten rid of staff. You do realize people are convinced that you're getting ready to sell the company?"

"Actually, today I'll be announcing my retirement." He glanced from daughter to son. "Congratulations. You two are now the new owners of Shields Corp."

FOURTEEN

Both Mark and Sunny leaped to their feet, but it was Sunny who found her voice first. "You mean we're supposed to *share* the company? But you can't! Mark doesn't deserve half of Shields Corp!"

"And I don't want it. Honestly, I don't." Mark could feel the old, familiar panic rising up his back, pouring tension into his shoulders. Was this his father's way to force him to his "rightful" role in the family company, whether he wanted it or not? Call a press conference? Announce to the world that Mark was now part owner of Shields Corp? Even if the tabloids hadn't exposed his identity, his father's press conference would have sent dozens of reporters scurrying to find the long-lost heir—and that was presuming his father wouldn't have inadvertently leaked the information himself—destroying TRUST's ability to fly under the radar. So much for thinking his father had changed. So much for everything Mark had done to escape the stigma of the Shields name. "Please, just give it all to Sunny."

"My decision is made." Jonah stood. "It will be an equal split. The paperwork has already been drawn up. As of tomorrow, the deal is done. I'm keeping this home and a small living allowance. The rest of the assets will be divided equally between the two of you with the exception of the main property, which you will share ownership of. Hopefully it's big enough for you to somehow share. But if not, Albright has the details of an interested buyer."

"But Dad—"

As the old, familiar name slipped across Mark's lips, the man's eyes met his, and Mark saw something there he'd never seen before. Sadness. The hard edge he was used to seeing was gone. Maybe his father wasn't trying to hurt him. Maybe he just didn't understand.

Mark took a deep breath and started again. "I appreciate the generosity, Dad, and I'm sure you must mean well. But I honestly love the work I'm doing now and don't want to give it up."

Jonah paused. His hand slipped over his chin as if willing his mouth to find the right words to say.

"Really," Mark added, "I don't want anything to do with the company."

Jonah's shoulders sagged. "Then tomorrow you are free to give your share to your sister. Although I hope you will at least consider sitting down with me tomorrow to discuss other possibilities. Now, if you'll excuse me, I have a press conference to give and a retirement party to enjoy." He glanced at each of them in turn. "I am hoping to see you there."

Jonah walked back into the other room and shut the door neatly behind him. Sunny turned to Mark and gaped like a fish that'd just been yanked out of water.

He put a hand on her slim shoulder. "It's okay, sis. We'll figure something out. Trust me."

She took a few shallow breaths. Then she shrugged off his arm without meeting his eye. "Come on. I'll give you a ride back to the main complex. I presume you'll want to get changed before the brunch. It sounds like it's going to be rather…memorable."

After a quick word with Detective Brant, they followed Sunny down the path to a yellow convertible. Mark opened the passenger door for Katie. Then he hopped in the back. Sunny slid into the driver's seat. She grabbed a pair of mirrored sunglasses from the glove compartment and snapped them on before pulling out. A police car was following at a respectable distance.

"Where's your bodyguard?" Mark asked.

Sunny tapped the soft flesh between her shoulder blades.

He felt a sudden wave of sympathy surge through him. "Really?" It had come to *that*?

"What?" Katie asked.

"I have a personalized GPS tracker implanted in my skin," Sunny said. "It monitors not only my location but my heart rate and vital signs." She glanced at Katie. "Go ahead and take a swing at me, and see how long it takes security to find me." She yanked on the steering wheel, swerving them around a corner and onto the main road. She gunned the engine and then grinned as the police escort disappeared in the distance.

"Oh, sis," Mark said. "I'm so sorry—"

"Why? That you weren't here to talk me out of it? Dad already tried." She glanced at Katie. "Do you know that when I was a kid my martial arts instructor kidnapped me? Ironic, right? The person my esteemed father hired to teach me how to protect myself threw me in the trunk of his car and left me in there for hours. I was six."

Katie's hand rose to her throat. "I'm…I'm so sorry."

"Yeah." Her voice was matter of fact. "Me, too. So don't blame me if I'm not about to trust my safety to a bodyguard. Anyway, as soon as the technology was available, my brother and I were expected to wear GPS everywhere we went. Twenty-four-seven, someone in a shiny metal room knew where we were. It started off as something we wore, but when the implants hit the market a couple of years ago, I upgraded." She glanced at her brother in the rearview mirror. "As you can imagine, it caused a pretty major stir when yours suddenly became active. That was one rescue I wanted to see myself."

They pulled up to the gates of Shields Corp. A guard waved them through. "Although our overall security staff has been reduced as part of Dad's big downsizing operation. We're down to a dozen or so. Yes, there's still a guard at the front gate, but the days of having a fleet of security patrolling the wider woods are long gone, and he hasn't had a personal bodyguard in ages. At least he seems to still know I'm worth protecting, even if he's stopped caring about whether random hikers walk on the edges of our property."

"I'm all for selling this place," she added. "It's hardly overflowing with happy memories for me. But you'll find it's not in the state you left it in. Dad's closed off three of the four main buildings. We're on a skeletal crew staff-wise. Ever since our grandmother died, Dad's been having some kind of spiritual crisis. He now insists on doing almost all the ground's work himself—which means over eighty percent of the green space has been left to go wild. No one has run a boat on the lake for so long the shoreline has gone back to its natural muddy state."

She glanced back at Katie. "You remember seeing the golf course and lake from the helicopter? It's outside the main complex. We used to host private tournaments on it for our company partners. We had thirty-six holes, not to mention the clubhouse. Now? No one's stepped foot there for years." She stopped sharply in front of the townhouse. "I trust you can find your way from here."

Mark hopped out and then opened the door for Katie. "Thanks for the ride."

His sister nodded curtly. For the first time in a long time, he felt the urge to hug his little sister and let her know that everything was going to be all right.

He sighed. "I'm sorry for leaving the way I did and not staying in touch. I never meant to leave you. I just needed a break from Dad and the company—and from all of this. I never meant to leave you behind."

Sunny stared at him for a moment. Her mouth set in a thin line. Her eyes stayed hidden behind sunglasses. "I would ask you what your intentions are, but really it doesn't matter. I deserve this company. I earned it. And one way or another, I'm going to end up with all of it. Even if it means suing you or convincing some lawyer that our father is not in his right mind and does not have the mental capacity to be making such a decision."

The car peeled off. Mark shook his head. "She doesn't trust me."

"It doesn't sound like she trusts anyone," Katie said.

Yeah, that was true enough. Did anyone in his small, fractured family actually trust each other? If only his father had told him he was planning on retiring and asked him if he'd wanted a share of the company. But it seemed that with a son who wouldn't answer his calls and a daughter who was so fiercely dedicated to looking out for herself, Jonah had just gone ahead and made the decision without them.

For a moment, he wondered what life must have been like from the other side of his father's desk. How must it have felt to pour his life into his work for so long only to wake up one day and realize the beast he'd created had swallowed up everyone and everything it touched?

It seemed no one liked what Shields Corp had become—including the Shieldses. Well, the most important thing to worry about now was doing whatever it took to make sure his own company was going to survive.

What had his father even been thinking offering him half of Shields Corp? And what was he going to do about it? He could still hear the voice of the angry young man he once was, urging him to throw the gift back in his father's face and leave. And yet, is that what he should do? After all, he'd come up here hoping to be able to squeeze a couple thousand dollars out of his father for the small island he'd gotten from his grandmother. If he could talk his sister into giving him something for his side of the company, it could make a huge difference to TRUST. But now that Katie's kidnappers had leaked his identity online, would it even be possible to keep the company going, or would his worst fears about being blacklisted come true? And if Sunny went through with her threat to sue, the bad publicity would ruin TRUST.

Not to mention, he still had a plane to catch.

"I need to find a lawyer," he said. "Someone who can get me out of this mess and sort things out while I'm overseas. Until I know how this is all going to play out, I should probably shut down the TRUST office for a while, really batten down the hatches and wait until all this blows over. The last thing I want is for the press to start chasing down people I know for comment. Or Nick to get caught up in an impending lawsuit when he's got a wedding to worry about. I'll disconnect the phones, tell Nick to take a few months off and tell everyone I've worked or associated with recently to keep their distance and watch their backs, including Zack. Should've really done that the moment I realized the kidnappers could link me to TRUST."

Katie turned to face him. Her hands brushed his arms. "What if the people who care about you want to go through this with you?"

He started to pull her in for a hug. But then he stopped himself and held her at arm's length. "I'm leaving the country the day after tomorrow. Won't be back for months. I don't want anyone putting their lives on hold waiting for me to get back."

"You make it sound like you're on your own in this. Like you're the one with the sole responsibility to be strong for everyone else." She rolled her shoulders back. He let her go. But to his surprise, instead of moving away, she stepped in closer, until he could almost feel her heart beating against his chest. "But you're not alone, Mark. People care about you. They respect you. They love you—because of who you are, not because of what name you were born with or who your father is. Let them choose if they want to go through this with you."

His body ached to reach out and wrap his arms around her. Instead, he stepped back. The more he acted on impulse, the greater the chance someone was going to get hurt. And right now, knowing she was okay was one of the few things still holding him together.

"I need to think." He slid the GPS medallion off his hand. Then taking her hands gently, he tied the GPS medallion onto her wrist. "Don't worry. You're safe here."

But her forehead wrinkled, and he watched as that courageous light that had lit up her eyes slowly dimmed to a shadow. Would he have even seen that light in her eyes or realized the extraordinary person she was if their lives hadn't been in danger? Now, there was a sobering thought. If it hadn't been for the unknown threat that'd been nipping at their heels since the moment they'd met, would he have ever given her a chance to get to know him? Or would he have just brushed her off, convinced she would never be able understand?

She shook her head. "It's not me I'm worried about."

He hugged her as quickly as he dared. Then he walked away without letting himself look back.

Katie twisted her hair into a bun and then grabbed a handful of bobby pins off the dresser so quickly she scratched herself. Tears rushed to her eyes. She blinked them back. No, she couldn't afford to let herself cry or she'd risk falling apart.

He had promised that he wouldn't shut her out again. But the moment stress hit, he had resorted to his default way of coping. Leaving. Pushing everyone else away. Trying to fix everything all on his own. Would someone like that ever be able to see her as an actual partner?

Whatever else Mark, Shields's security and the police were doing, she wasn't going to let herself get caught unprepared again. She stepped back and ran a critical eye over her outfit. She'd chosen a simple brown-and-white silk sundress and matched it with a pale cream blazer. The final effect was crisp, clean and professional enough for a brunch. But the skirt was full enough that she'd managed to hide a pair of hiking shorts underneath just in case something went terribly wrong and she needed to run.

For a moment, her eyes were drawn to a delicate pair of white strappy sandals. But instead, she chose a pair of wedge-heeled ankle boots with sturdy laces and good soles.

She slipped a small pair of scissors, a nail file, the remains of her phone and Mark's wrist GPS into the blazer's inside pocket. Not much in terms of weaponry, but if he had taught her anything, it was to not underestimate the little things. It never hurt to be prepared. A slight smile crossed her lips. She really was beginning to sound like him.

There was a flurry of knocking at the front door. Hard. Insistent. *Please let it be Mark—*

She hurried into the living room as the knocking grew louder. She grabbed the handle. The door flew open.

"Hello, gorgeous. Don't just stand there. Gimme a hug."

Katie felt her mouth fall open. It was Ethan.

"Surprise!" His grin was manic. He saw the look of shock on her face and practically rubbed his hands together. "So no one tipped you off I was coming. Awesome-sauce." The boyish mop of hair seemed even messier than usual, and there were dark circles under his pale eyes. He was wearing a rumpled designer suit with a garish turquoise tie. "You gonna let me in?"

She pulled back the lock and opened the door.

"Hey." She forced a smile so tight she could feel the pinch in her cheeks. "What are you doing here? How did you even get past security?"

"I just showed them my press credentials and a printout of the press invitation-thingy they sent us." He shot her a withering glance. "I am your boss, after all, and the editor of a pretty important publication."

She fought the urge to roll her eyes. Calling *Impact* important was a bit of a stretch. He walked past her into the living room, dumping a large black duffel bag just inside the doorway, like he was expecting someone to put it away for him. Right, well as soon as brunch was over she'd ask Albright to direct him to find a suitable hotel.

"Figured you could use some company for the party tonight." He collapsed sideways into a chair. "Should be epic."

Huh. Judging by what she'd seen of Jonah, it was hardly going to be the kind of wild party Ethan would be after. She'd have an easier time believing the "Mark Armor Is Jonah Shields Junior" story was getting a lot of media attention, and Ethan was there hoping to personally take credit for an exclusive. Then again, he might honestly be looking for a new crowd of people to charm because there wasn't anything interesting going on in Toronto. You never could tell once he had an idea in his head.

"Got anything to drink?"

"The brunch is starting in about fifteen minutes. I'm sure there'll have plenty of both juice and coffee."

He frowned. "I meant a real drink."

Oh, she knew exactly what he meant. "Why are you here, again?"

"I flew up this morning. A friend of mine has a helicopter. This whole cat-and-mouse thing you've got going on is turning into the biggest story we've ever had. One of our own writers actually survived a kidnapping attempt—"

He didn't even know the half of it.

"—and I couldn't risk you mismanaging it any further."

Mismanaging it? She turned toward the window and closed her eyes for a moment. *Remember, this is a man who only cares about himself. Don't let yourself get dragged down to his level.* "So does that mean you're going to be writing this story now?"

"No." He chuckled. "I thought I'd leave that part up to your expertise." His eyes scanned her in a way she guessed was meant to be flirtatious but instead was almost threatening. "You are very, very important to *Impact News* and to me. It's about time we get this story back on track."

About fifty journalists from various news outlets had shown up for the brunch, along with another thirty or so distinguished guests. According to the papers she'd received from Albright, they were expecting closer to five hundred people for the gala tonight. Apparently, if Jonah Shields was stepping down, he was doing so with style. His speech had been simple and given without notes. Jonah was thankful for all God had given him but was ready to step down, so he was splitting the company between his two children—Mark and Sunny. Katie was oddly surprised to hear him mention God and also thankful that he respected Mark enough not to call him Junior or mention TRUST.

She'd caught sight of Mark hanging in the doorway when the speech began. But he'd slipped out the moment his father stepped away from the microphone. He hadn't once looked her way or indicated he wanted to talk. She resisted the urge to follow.

Jonah refused to take public questions and instead directed them to Albright. About thirty reporters charged toward the private secretary. The other twenty ran for Sunny. Katie stood in the back and tried to find the appetite to eat.

Sunny was glad-handing everyone within sight, looking every bit the competent heiress ready to lead the company. "Oh, I don't think anyone knows what my brother's been doing honestly. Wandering around from resort to resort on some vanity project I imagine—"

"Excuse me." Katie stepped calmly but firmly between Sunny and the closest microphone.

Sunny stopped and held up a hand. The media stepped back. Sunny gestured her away from the crowd.

"What is your problem?" Sunny hissed. "If you're after an interview, I promise that, considering your unique circumstances, I will be happy to give you an exclusive interview at a later time once my lawyer has drawn up a suitable confidentiality agreement on what you can and can't—"

"I don't care about that," Katie said, surprised to realize how true it really was. "I care about Mark."

Sunny opened her mouth, but Katie didn't pause long enough to let her in.

"Look. I know you and your brother have a history, and I'm sure he's made his fair share of mistakes. But please don't undermine the work he's done. Did you know he's been giving everything he has to actually saving the lives of others?"

Sunny's eyes widened. She shook her head.

"His company—TRUST—provides electricity to hospitals and clean drinking water to orphanages. The broadcast transmitter he created has the potential to save countless lives. I don't blame you if you hate him, but please don't hurt those whose lives he's worked hard to save. Please." She stepped back, her heart beating like a warrior's drum in her chest.

For a minute, Sunny just stood there, stunned,

until a reporter approached and tapped her on the shoulder. Katie expected her to snap back into professional action, but instead, she shook her head, waved the reporter away and walked out of the tent.

Just when she thought she had Mark's sister figured out, Sunny threw her a curveball.

"What did you say to her?"

She turned, barely seeing the man beside her except for the large microphone he was shoving in her face.

"Excuse me." She followed Sunny's lead and headed out of the tent. Thankfully, the reporter didn't follow. The green was empty. Truth be told, she didn't blame Sunny for being angry. Her mother had died when she was young. She'd survived a terrible kidnapping shortly after that and grown up with a father too preoccupied and distant to help her through it. No wonder she'd seen Mark's leaving as a betrayal. It was amazing she hadn't tried to disrupt her father's event.

She sat down on a bench. A dark thought crossed Katie's mind. What if Sunny had? After all, she had more to gain than anyone by ruining both her father's and brother's reputations. But if so, why risk the kidnapping to a ragtag bunch of thugs? And why link it back to one of Shields Corp's worst public relations disasters? Surely, Sunny was far too smart to try a scheme so far-fetched and ham-fisted.

She heard someone call her name and sighed.

Ethan was loping in her direction. Somehow his suit managed to look even more rumpled than before. His breath stank, and he was grinning. He seemed to have dropped his bag somewhere. She'd refused to let him leave it in her room.

"I got us a helicopter tour of the area. Figured we could buzz around and get the aerial view."

"Actually, I did that yesterday. So, if it's all the same to you I'll sit this one out."

"Oh, come on." He tugged on her arm. "One more spin around here isn't going to hurt you any."

"I promised a friend that I wouldn't go far."

He scowled. "Since when does someone other than me dictate what you do on an assignment? I'm really not liking this new side of you. I don't know what's changed, but it's like you're forgetting who's your boss." Then the smile was back again as quickly as it had gone. "Now, hurry up. We're not leaving the area. We're just flying around it."

Fair enough. Mark might be a while, and she did still have his GPS bracelet on her. She stood slowly, taking in a strong and sudden whiff of his breath. "You've been drinking, haven't you?"

He shook his head, vigorously.

Sure. "I'm not going anywhere with you if you're not sober."

"I'm not drunk. And it's not like I'm going to be the one flying the helicopter."

Right. She followed as he bounded his way down

to the helipad. It could be hard to tell when he had actually been taking something or just was suffering the residual effects from years of substance abuse. The way his mood could rapidly shift was nerve-racking.

She grit her teeth together. In just three months' time she'd get her chance to convince the board that she should have his job. But the reminder of that left her feeling hollow. Writing all those articles to one day show the board had given her a sense of control, of power, like she was building something she could be proud of. But at what cost? Did she really want a job that had cost her the chance at a life? Once she'd sent her life hurtling down the path of long days and no sleep, always chasing after that next deadline, would it ever actually stop?

A sudden grin crossed her face. Funny, the thought of losing her job had her practically paralyzed a few days ago. Now she was seriously considering quitting.

Mark held the phone to his ear and waited as Zack's answering machine went through its recorded message. There was a beep. He paused.

On the long walk he'd taken before heading back to the privacy of his own guest townhouse, he'd carefully rehearsed the message he intended to leave. The garage in Kapuskasing had given Zack's motorcycle a clean bill of health. Mark had given them what little remained on his credit card. He would get it to Zack before heading to the airport. The plan was to keep the exchange brief and friendly—leaving out everything about the latest attempt on his life, not to mention his father's overwhelming, unwanted gift and his sister's threatened lawsuit.

But somehow Katie's plea not to shut people out had pricked at the edges of his mind. He was actually trying to protect his former bodyguard now—just like he was trying to protect his colleagues and Katie. For years, he'd tried to convince himself he was protecting his father from an unpleasant conversation by not returning his calls. He'd even thought he'd been protecting Sunny by hiding all his doubts and frustrations from her and choosing instead just to walk away.

The machine cut off. He set the phone back down.

The small gray helicopter was about half the size of the one Katie had been rescued by the day before. The pilot barely nodded to them as they climbed in.

"You hired this?"

"Yup." Ethan dropped into the seat. "I hire them all the time. Beats a limo hands down when you want to make an entrance. Of course, half the time you can't find anywhere to land them. But even so, it's still cool."

Ethan's bragging about the various ways he liked to waste money was yet another one of those things that she'd just gotten used to in the office. But here, his bravado seemed almost laughable. Despite the problems Mark, Sunny and their father had about the division of the company, at least you couldn't accuse them of taking their troubles lightly.

She slid the aircraft headset over her ears and then reached down to close the door.

"Hey, Katie! Wait up." Mark was sprinting toward them.

She tapped the pilot on the shoulder. "Hang on."

"Who's that?" Ethan glanced past her. "He can't come. I've got something really special planned, and I don't want him messing it up."

Special? Katie almost snorted. He'd better not have planned on doing anything inappropriate. She'd heard rumors of her boss tagging along on business trips with other female colleagues before.

"Let's go." Ethan smacked the back of the pilot's seat. "Leave him!"

Mark ducked his head under the propellers. "Don't tell me you're leaving already."

"No. Nothing like that. Ethan, my boss, just showed up and wanted a tour."

"Nice to meet you, Ethan. I'm Mark."

Ethan sniffed and turned toward the window. Did he not recognize Mark? Or was he too drunk to care?

Mark shrugged. "Okay then. Katie, I'll see you when you get back."

"No, wait." She grabbed his hand. "How about you come with us?" If she was going to be stuck in a small metal compartment with her drunken, lecherous boss, it was better not to have to do it alone.

She tilted her head toward Ethan just enough to make sure Mark caught the gesture. "Please. We would enjoy the extra company."

"No, we would not." Ethan turned back. His hand landed on her leg in a gesture that was both possessive and unpleasant. "Katie, this is a business trip, not a joyride."

Mark's eyes moved seamlessly from Ethan's hand to Katie's face. Then he stepped up into the helicopter. "I'm sorry. I'm afraid we got off on the wrong foot." He extended his hand toward Ethan. Ethan took his hand off Katie and crossed his arms. "I am Jonah Shields's son. I grew up here and know the area better than anyone. On behalf of the Shields Corporation, I'd be happy to give you a guided tour."

Thank you, God. How could Ethan possibly say no to that?

He didn't bother trying. Instead, Ethan looked Mark up and down like some horse he was considering buying. Then he nodded. "All right." Ethan climbed into the front seat and shoved a headset over his ears.

Mark slid onto the seat beside her and reached for a headset. She smiled at him gratefully. While *Impact* had already splashed his identity across their website, she couldn't imagine introducing himself as Jonah's son to a tabloid editor had been comfortable. They fastened their seat belts. Ethan didn't even reach for his.

She tapped him on his shoulder. "You're going to want to buckle up."

No response. Oh, great, he was sulking.

As the helicopter rose, the heavy strum of the propellers filled the small metal space. The soundproofing must have been heavy in the Shields helicopter for her and Sunny to have been able to talk in normal decibels without headsets.

She turned to Mark, careful to remember that even though Ethan's back was to them, the headsets meant he'd still be able to hear every word. "Make your calls?"

He shook his head. "Not yet. Mostly walked and prayed."

The pilot seemed to be idly flying large loops around the forest, as if waiting for Ethan to tell him where to go. She almost laughed. Back in the office, they'd learned to worry whenever he was silent. Now, what was the worst he could do to her? Even if he fired her the moment they landed, she was fairly sure Sunny and Jonah would both still honor the promise of giving her an exclusive. If Mark was all right with her doing it, she could sell it as a freelancer. If not, then Ethan would've fired her anyway for honoring Mark's feelings.

As they soared through a break in the trees, the long, winding road leading to the Shields complex spread out beneath them. Verses from Psalm 139 fluttered to the front of her mind. *"You hem me in behind and before, and you lay your hand upon me. Such knowledge is too lofty for me to attain..."*

There was a black van underneath them speeding toward the complex. A special guest who was late for the brunch or early for the gala that night? Or just a delivery van of some sort? A sudden chill spread through her limbs, and she slid closer to Mark. The last time she'd been too close to a delivery van she'd been lucky to make it out alive. She took a deep breath and centered herself.

"Where can I go from your Spirit? Where can I flee from your presence?"

"Hey, man." Mark tapped the pilot on the shoulder. "You're flying a bit low. You might want to pull up a bit, or you'll risk clipping a tree." The pilot shrugged and ignored him.

The road dipped sharply to the left. The van swerved hard and barely managed to stay out of the ditch. Chances were the driver had been too busy watching the helicopter to notice where the road was going.

"If I go up to the heavens you are there... If I make my bed in the depths..."

As she watched, the van below them skid into a tree, and a deafening bang filled the air. The van burst into flames. Ethan swore loudly. Panic gripped at Katie's throat as she looked down to see the vehicle's windows explode outward. Thick black smoke billowed out of the back. Tongues of fire licked out through the van's shattered windows.

The delivery vehicle had just caught fire. But how? Why? How did a van just blow up like that? And why were the flames coming out of the back and not the engine?

Mark's hand grabbed hers. His face had gone white. "I think they were carrying some kind of crude explosive device."

"What?" Her mind scrambled to make sense of what he was telling her.

"I think the van contained some kind of homemade bomb. And it went off."

Smoke from the fire below began to fill the air around them. The helicopter pilot peered out the window, craning his neck to look at the fire below. Ethan was shaking.

"Stop gawking." Mark banged hard on the back of pilot's seat. "We've got to get away from here! Now!"

But it was too late. Within moments, smoke had surrounded the small aircraft, blocking their view from the windows on every side. The pilot swore and grabbed for the controls. He was flying blind. Fear gripped Katie's throat. If he couldn't see, they couldn't land. "I'm just going to—" But the pilot's words were lost in the crack of tree branches hitting the sides of the helicopter. The nose of the aircraft dipped sharply toward the ground. Mark threw his arms around her and pulled them both down into the brace position. She closed her eyes, panicked prayers pouring from her lungs.

They were going to crash.

FIFTEEN

Pain exploded through Katie's head like stars. A heavy mass of trees had broken the helicopter's fall. The small aircraft was now suspended sideways, caught between two trees a few feet off the ground.

"You okay?" Mark's hand was still clutching hers like a lifeline.

"I think so." *Thank God.* She looked around, her eyes struggling to make sense of the scene around her. Ethan had been tossed between the front seats and was now wedged there. Blood was smeared against the console and splashed up against the windscreen. The pilot wasn't moving.

Mark kicked the door open. They had stopped about eight feet off the ground. The branches had cushioned their fall; otherwise there was no telling how fast they would've hit the ground. He swung his legs into the gap, unbuckled his seat belt and then dropped down onto the forest floor. Then he reached up for her. "Can you get your seat belt off?"

"Yes. But what about the others?"

"Once you're out, I'll climb back in and we can see about getting them out."

She struggled against the seat belt for a moment; then suddenly, it swung free. She fell a couple of feet before feeling his hand reach up to steady her. She jumped down. Thick trees filled her view in every direction.

Mark hauled himself back in. "Your boss is alive. But unconscious. If I lower him down, can you help him onto the ground?"

"Yeah."

Slowly, Ethan's feet and legs came into view. She wrapped her arms around his waist, then carefully eased him onto the ground. Mark tossed down a pillow. She tucked it under his head. Ethan groaned.

There was a long pause, and then Mark leaped back down to the ground again. "The pilot's dead. He smashed his head against the console. Death would have been immediate. Probably never even knew what had happened."

She pressed her fingers into her temples. "There was a delivery van on the road below us, and then it exploded." Her head was still throbbing. "You said you thought it was a bomb?"

"A homemade, badly constructed one, yes." He slid an arm around her shoulder. "It's just a guess. But it's an educated one. Especially since Detective Brandt mentioned bomb-making sites this morning. I'd hazard, something in a glass container that broke when they hit the corner. I once helped clear a clinic in Africa after rebels had mined it with handmade explosives. Crude, sloppy, small radius, but they can still pack a pretty powerful punch."

Ethan muttered something that sounded like "online now" before lapsing into a string of unintelligible gibberish.

Mark wrinkled his nose. "Has he been drinking?"

"Probably alcohol plus drugs of some sort. It's an everyday thing with him."

"I'm sorry. It must make him horrible to work for." He knelt down and pried Ethan's eyes open long enough to get the pupil size. Ethan whined and threatened to kill him. Then he started snoring as soon as Mark let him go. "I'm guessing he has a concussion. But I can't tell if it's anything more serious than that until the drugs wear off. We've got to get him to a hospital."

He felt in Ethan's pockets and pulled out a cell phone. It fell apart in his hands. "The pilot's phone didn't survive the crash either, and the radio is down. You still got my GPS?"

She dug it out of her pocket. The medallion was so badly dented it was bent almost in half. She dropped it into his hand. He ran his fingers over the twisted metal. He shook his head. "I can't activate the emergency signal. But hopefully the GPS is still emitting. Can you walk?"

She nodded.

"Hopefully we're not that far from the road."

His eyes fell onto her face. "What is it?"

She stepped forward and kissed him on the cheek. "I'm just really thankful you're here right now."

"There's nowhere else I'd rather be." He looked back at the wall of trees and chuckled under his breath. "Well, obviously there are a lot of places I'd rather we were right now. But yeah, when the explosion went off, I was thanking God pretty hard that we were in this together."

He slid his arms under Ethan and scooped him up like a child. Ethan moaned something unintelligible and swatted at him ineffectually.

There was the crack of breaking branches off to her right, followed by the rustle of something moving through the trees. "Someone's coming."

"Actually, sounds more like a team of someone's." He pulled Ethan's limp body to his chest. "Looks like someone saw our helicopter go down and sent out a search party."

The trees parted. Al stepped into the clearing. Billy and the two other young men she'd seen on the highway flanked him.

Al cocked a handgun and pointed it straight at Mark's head. "This time we're going to do things my way."

SIXTEEN

Maybe it would have been different if it hadn't been for the gun in Al's hand. Maybe if she hadn't seen the motley group of armed young men behind him or known that Mark was holding Ethan's semidelirious body…maybe then the fight instinct would have kicked in for Katie. Maybe she would have grabbed the nearest heavy object, barreled into Al screaming at the top of her lungs and fought for their lives. At least that's what she'd end up telling herself on the nights she couldn't sleep. But it all happened so fast. Al and his makeshift army had Mark surrounded before he could have possibly set Ethan down safely.

"Katie!" Mark shouted. "Run!"

But before she could take two steps, Billy's hand had clamped on her wrist, yanking her back. Desperately, she grabbed his arm with her other hand and tried to twist herself out of his grasp when the sudden sound of gunfire filled the air.

One of the boys had fired. Yanking her arm free, she spun toward Mark, relief coursing through her when she saw he was still standing. Al turned slowly toward his army, keeping his gun trained on Mark's head.

The boys were looking to Al with hesitation. They were all teenagers, and one seemed so drunk he could barely stand up straight. An assortment of different guns and knives were in their hands.

So this is what you got by placing an ad online— stupid, young, angry, desperate thugs who weren't even sure what they were supposed to be shooting at. Al was old enough to have chosen this kind of evil. But what about his followers? The kidnapper the police already had in custody was young enough to still be in high school. How old had the driver of the van been?

"Let them go." She stepped in front of him. "These kids? Let them all go, and please get my friend Ethan to a hospital. I don't know what you're after, but nobody else needs to die for it. I'll stay—"

"No!" Mark slowly lowered Ethan to the ground. He opened his hands and held them palms up. "Take me. Let Katie and everyone else go."

A hideous grin stretched across Al's face.

Desperately, Katie's eyes met Mark's. She mouthed, "I don't want to leave you." He shook his head.

"Katie has done nothing to deserve this." Mark turned back to their kidnappers. "I don't know why you're after her, but I promise you that you've got the wrong woman." He took a step forward. "I'm Jonah Shields's son. Whatever problem you think you have with the Shields Corp or whatever money you're hoping to collect, take me instead. I promise if you guarantee her safety I will not fight you."

"Do you think I'm stupid?" Al snapped. "You so much as flinch and I'll shoot off her hand. Keep fighting me after that and I'll take off the other one, then feet and then I'll start to get really creative." He chuckled. "I just need her alive. I don't care what state she's in."

He flicked a hand toward the boys. They moved around her and encircled her. A skinny figure stepped forward and pushed the butt of his gun into her neck.

She glanced at the boy, staring into his young brown eyes. "Please. I don't know what lies you've been told. But believe me. You're not going to get what you want this way."

Al snorted and shot her a withering glance. "I can assure you that by the time this is done I will have exactly what I want." He'd stepped toward her, reached down and grabbed her by the hair, turning her face until it was looking directly into his own. "I've been promised a lot of money for you, and believe me, if I had known how much trouble you were going to be, I would have asked for double. Now that I have you, I am not about to let you go until I have collected every penny." He glanced at Mark. "Then I'll worry about what I can get for him."

She winced as the pain of his grip shot through her skull.

"I'm warning you," she gasped, "that no matter what you threaten us with, we're not going to make it easy for you."

His laugh turned into a snarl. Someone yanked her hands together from behind. She heard Mark shout. Then something was pulled over her head.

Mark's heart was beating so hard he could feel each painful beat as it banged against his chest. He watched as the boys pulled a pillowcase over Katie's head. Then they bound her hands behind her back with a zip tie.

Oh, God, what do I do?

Everything in him wanted to charge the men and fight them for her life. But he also knew sudden movement could get Katie shot.

Katie kicked and thrashed as two of the boys tried to grab her legs. Al had only three teenagers with him now. None of the boys looked strong enough to carry Katie by themselves, and there was no way they'd be able to carry all three of them.

"Let her walk," Mark shouted, "or are you planning to carry us all that way?"

Al held up a hand. Katie stopped kicking and went limp.

Good job. As long as they left her legs untied, there was a chance she could still run. A slim chance, but he'd take anything that increased her chances of survival. Ethan groaned and crawled onto his hands and knees. Grabbing on to Mark, he dragged himself to his feet like a toddler leaning on a parent.

Al smirked. "Fine." He gestured to Ethan. "You help Billy carry that one. I'm sure I can find use for another hostage. If you put him down, I will shoot her. If you do not walk where I tell you, I will shoot her. If either of you try to run, I will shoot her."

Mark nodded and slid an arm under Ethan's shoulder. At least he wasn't being asked to let Ethan die. No matter what he had been like as a boss, no one deserved that.

One of the boys yanked a pillowcase over Mark's head. Then Al instructed them to march. Mark stepped forward, shrugging his shoulders just lightly enough to create a millimeter gap between the pillowcase and his chest. Okay, now he could see the ground.

They were walking through the forest. He and Billy were half dragging, half carrying Katie's boss as he stumbled along between them. Hands shoved Mark forward. A rifle butt jabbed hard into the small of his back. Mark kept his breath steady, focused on the patch of ground at his feet, and he listened for the sound of Katie's breath. As Zack had often pointed out, patience had never come easily to him. His impulse was to run, to fight and to jump into action without thinking. Much as he'd left home without even thinking through how it would hurt his sister.

Now, if he started running recklessly, he was risking the life of someone he loved.

Okay, God. I'm listening. Waiting on you.

One of the boys was arguing with Al now. It was apparent he was having second thoughts. But when Al threatened to shoot him, the boy fell silent again.

It was clear who was the boss of this operation. And he was either foolish enough or greedy enough to take more hostages than he could probably manage to ransom. But Al's methods had been sloppy from the beginning, and his mistakes might have been all that had kept them alive so far. It was also clear from what Al had said earlier that he'd been acting on the orders of someone else. Someone else wanted Katie kidnapped. Al was just the hired gun.

Tell me what to do. Tell me how to save her. Show me when to act.

The gun barrel pushed him forward. He focused on the tiny gaps of terrain at his feet. Judging by the scuff marks, they were tracing the same ground the men had walked to find them. The ground sloped down slightly. He heard the soft lapping of water brushing the shore. Then suddenly, they left the woods and stepped out onto soft green turf.

The golf course. Oh, thank you, God. He knew where they were.

They followed the grass until it turned to cobblestone. Of course, the abandoned clubhouse. It was outside the main walls, and from what Sunny had said, it was unlikely Shields's security would be wasting their manpower on monitoring it too closely.

Their kidnappers propelled them up a flight of wide stone steps and through the front lobby. *Come on, Mark, think. You've got this. You know where you are.* Ethan was yanked from his grasp, and Mark heard him cry out in pain. Then his voice disappeared behind a slamming door. So Al was separating them. Mark focused on Katie's breath, fast and shallow and just a few steps ahead of him. They turned right, down a hallway, through a door and then up another flight of stairs to the service level.

A door creaked open to his right. The storage closet. Of course. The claustrophobic space with built-in shelves probably looked like the perfect makeshift cell.

At least, to an inattentive eye.

"Stick her in there," Al said. "We'll put him in the freezer."

He heard Katie gasp and then the sound of her falling. *Dear Lord, please give me the speed.* Mark yanked the pillowcase off his head and dove toward the storage cupboard. The teenager behind him fumbled with his gun, then fired, the bullet flying so close to Mark's back he half expected to feel the searing pain of a bullet pierce his skin. Instead, the recoil seemed to have thrown the boy off balance, sending the bullet into the door frame. Pushing Katie in deeper, Mark slammed the heavy door behind them and braced his weight against it. Dim light was filtering in through a skylight high above. Yanking his belt off, he wrapped it around the inside door latch and tethered it to the built-in shelves.

There, that should keep them from being able to open the door until he could think of a more permanent solution.

There was the sound of Al yelling, the door rattling, the hammer being yanked back on a gun. Mark threw his body over Katie's as someone started firing into the cupboard. The metal door was pretty strong, but it would hardly hold up forever under that kind of punishment.

"Stop!" Al ordered. "You're wasting ammo." The bullets stopped. "They're not going anywhere. You there, watch the door and keep your gun pointed at it."

Mark rolled off Katie. "It's okay. It's me. We're safe." Pulling her into his arms, he eased the pillowcase off Katie's head.

She choked back a sob and fell against his chest. "Where are we?"

"We're in a storage closet in the golf clubhouse."

"And Ethan?"

"I don't know. They left him downstairs. My biggest fear was that they were going to separate us, too." So afraid, in fact, that he'd risked diving for the closet while he still had a gun to his back. If their kidnappers had been professionals, he'd be dead by now.

He followed her eyes as they scanned from the door to metal shelves, mostly bare but for a few half-empty bottles of cleaning solution.

"How do we get out of here?"

"We climb." He pointed up. "Up the shelves and through the skylight. Hopefully. If that fails, I start disassembling the shelves, make something we can protect ourselves with and then break down the door. Chances are, whoever tried shooting it did us a favor by weakening it. But I'd rather try to make it out of here without anyone else getting hurt."

He shook his head. What kind of amateur tried to kidnap someone on their home turf? He sat back against the shelf. Then he helped her sit up with her back to him. "I locked myself in here once when I was ten. Just to irritate the bodyguard they'd assigned to me. I knew every corner of this place when I was a kid. If the bolt can't slide back all the way, the door won't open. So, I'd just wedged bungee cord around it, fastened it to the shelf and then climbed up through one of the skylights. By the time they managed to break the door down, I was halfway to Kapuskasing. Of course, I'd brought a screwdriver in with me," he looked up, "and I was a lot smaller then."

He slid his fingers down her arms and into the plastic zip tie binding her wrists.

"I've got scissors," she said, "and a nail file in my pocket."

He grinned and brushed a kiss over her hairline. "You are amazing."

She shrugged the jacket off one shoulder and helped him spill the contents out onto the floor. Her broken cell phone hit the floor with a crack— the case splitting in two. "You're still carrying your phone?"

"I'm hoping to be able to transfer the memory into another phone."

"Well, I can—" He paused. Something was blinking inside the case. But there was no way the phone should still be getting a signal. "Do you mind if I break this case open?"

"Go ahead."

It came apart in his hands. He spilled the contents out onto his palm. And then he breathed in sharply. "Where did you get this phone?"

"Work. Why?"

"Someone's been tracking you by GPS."

SEVENTEEN

Katie leaned back against Mark inside the storage closet and waited as he cut at her bonds with the scissors. The plastic was thick, and the scissors were tiny, but already she could feel her wrists moving more freely.

"Someone installed a GPS tracker in my phone? No wonder they were always able to find me. On the road, at that rest stop, even in the woods—they were probably tracking my every move. But if they could track me, why go to all the trouble of taking out the train tracks in Cobalt? And how something like that got in my phone, I have no idea. I've only had it a couple of weeks, and it's practically been on me the whole time since then."

His fingers brushed against the inside of her wrists, pulling at her bonds, before going back to cutting. "The GPS was really badly installed. If I had to guess, it was installed by someone who didn't know how to use a screwdriver and was following online instructions."

Maybe that explained why the phone had never really worked properly.

"I'd almost be tempted to think that Al or Billy installed it," he said. "Except, why would they bother if they'd already kidnapped you? This whole thing has been so sloppy."

Sloppy. That was a good word for it. Haphazard. Disorganized. Amateur.

"Every instinct in my body is telling me that we're not dealing with professional criminals. Just a bunch of wannabes."

Someone decided to kidnap her. So they hired Al who, while both vicious and evil, hardly seemed to be a professional kidnapper. Then he, or whoever he was hired by, placed an advertisement on a website looking for new recruits—a move so risky, so public, it was almost laughable. Anyone could have seen it.

Then when he finally got her in his grasp, he didn't even take her back to whoever hired him, let alone to somewhere secluded. Instead, he took his prisoners onto Shields's property. It was almost like their captors were hoping to get noticed. She could feel the questions ticking in the back of her mind, like an ignition waiting to spark.

Already the sunlight slipping through the skylight seemed dimmer. Had anyone seen the helicopter go down? Would they know where to look for them? Even if someone was still monitoring his GPS, they'd probably just think Mark had gone for a stroll to check up on the gift his father had bestowed on him.

Yeah, they had to hope their kidnappers had missed the news that his father just gave him half the company.

She shivered.

"Cold?" he said.

"Just thinking." The plastic snapped off her wrists. She pulled her arms around in front of her and rolled her shoulders. "Thank you."

"You're welcome," he said. "Get used to feeling your arms again, and then we'll worry about getting out of here."

He climbed up the metal shelving like a ladder and then braced himself against the skylight.

"Any luck?"

"It's screwed shut." He grinned. "But thankfully you brought me a nail file."

She stood and stretched her arms out in front of her carefully. Then she stretched her legs and her back. Like an athlete getting ready for a race.

A screw tumbled onto the ground beside her.

"Easy as cutting a cake."

She glanced up. "You sure we're going to be able to fit through there?"

"Trust me. It'll be fine."

Right. Trust. They still hadn't heard a peep from outside the door. She didn't want to guess what might be happening to Ethan. She shut her eyes tight and whispered a prayer for his safety. Hopefully, they had just dumped him somewhere to sober up. "If we make it out of here safely—"

"When." A second screw fell.

She smiled. "When we make it out of here, Ethan is going to run straight for the telephones. The coverage he gave to my kidnapping earlier is hardly going to compare to the downright media frenzy he'll try to whip up now." She frowned. "It's horrible. Through everything that's happened, it was like he didn't care one iota about what I might be going through. The only thing he thought about was what a big story this would be."

But the media was like this whenever human tragedy struck. As it was, this whole kidnapping fiasco was practically just a badly written manifesto away from being a publicity stunt.

Then an idea shot across her mind and caught fire. Could it all be that simple? "Mark!"

Another screw fell. "Hang on. I nearly got this." He pocketed the last screw and then pounded on the skylight until it opened. He stuck his head outside and took in a deep breath of air. Then he jumped back down beside her. "You ready to climb?"

"More than ready, and I think I actually have a theory about what's going on now, or at least half a theory. I'll tell you once we're out of here."

She reached up to climb, but he placed a hand on her shoulder.

"Tell me now." There was something in his voice she couldn't quite place.

"You okay?"

His fingers slid up onto her shoulders and along her neck, stroked the soft skin under her hairline. "Yeah," he said gruffly. "Tell me your theory."

She took a deep breath, surprised to feel it prickle painfully inside her chest. "I haven't been thinking about this like a journalist. Really, the fact someone took pictures and then sent them to the tabloids should have been a red flag. Imagine you were a stupid, reckless, small-time criminal looking to get famous overnight. What would you do?"

"Some kind of stunt," he said. "Something violent and shocking, like kidnapping or killing someone. If pulling off some kind of large-scale attack wasn't feasible, then the goal would be to nab someone who'd practically guarantee you media coverage."

"Like a reporter—and now also an editor—from a small, gossipy publication that is hungry for scandal."

He leaned his forehead against hers. "You're brilliant, you know that?"

"It's just a theory."

He curled her hair around his fingers. "But it's a good one. Angry, evil idiots have been kidnapping journalists overseas for decades, just to get their point across."

"Except, in this case, we have no clue what their point is—"

Someone banged hard on the metal door with such force the noise seemed to shake the air. "Open the door." It was Al.

Mark cupped his hands underneath her head and tilted her face until she was looking directly into his. "Climb. Now."

"I promise you we have ways of making you open this door," Al shouted.

"Listen." Mark slid a finger over her lips. "I will not fit through that hole. You will."

She could feel tears pushing their way to the corner of her eyes. No. Not like this. She couldn't just leave him. There was another hard knock on the other side of the door. Her face turned. Their kidnappers were laughing.

"Don't worry." He guided her face back to his. "I'll be fine. I can take the shelves apart, and I'll go through the odds and ends stored in here for anything I can use to defend myself. That's presuming they even manage to break in before you come back with help."

"But if we hold them off together—"

"Then you could get hurt, and no one will even know that we're out here." He slipped his lips over hers. "I trust you. I know you'll make it. I know you'll come back for me. Now, trust me."

But she couldn't. She cared about him too much

to leave him. Not here. Not now. Wherever he was, she wanted to be—

A voice cried out in pain. Mark's face went pale. "Oh, God," he breathed, "Please no…"

"As you can hear," Al said, "I have your father."

Katie's hands slipped on the metal shelf as she scrambled up toward the skylight. Beneath her, she could hear Mark beginning to untie the door. He wouldn't open it until he knew she was clear, even though with every passing second he faced the fear of what the kidnappers might be doing to Jonah.

She reached the top shelf and slid her arms through the open window and out into the fresh air. It was so tight a squeeze that she almost didn't make it. But then, with a desperate shove, she propelled herself out onto the roof.

Beneath her she could hear the sound of the door opening, her heart breaking as she heard Mark calling out to his injured father. Al was swearing. He was threatening to hurt them both unless they told him where she had gone. Then she heard the sound of someone else climbing up the metal shelving.

She ran across the roof, her eyes scanning desperately for a way to get down. She reached the edge of the roof. The lake spread out in one direction and the golf course in the other. There was a wide stone balcony beneath her with a long, weathered canopy stretching out above it. She looked back.

None of Al's army had been thin enough to follow her through, but they'd be sure to come for her
some other way. She climbed down onto the canopy and slithered across on her hands and knees.
Then she swung over the edge and down onto the
balcony below.

*Oh, Lord, you are familiar with all my ways...
even when I can't figure out which way I'm supposed to go.*

She pressed her palm against the sliding glass
door, breathing a sigh of relief when it slid open in
front of her. Almost instantly, she heard the sound of
a gun cocking. Billy was standing behind a desk in
the dark, wood-paneled lounge. Mark's radio transmitter lay open in front of him. "Show me how to
run this thing." With a shaky hand, he pointed the
gun at her head. "Or I will make you pay."

EIGHTEEN

Mark leaned back against the metal shelves and looked over at the old man sitting on the floor opposite him. It was ironic. For as long as he could remember, his father had been larger than life. Now, sitting, captured on a hard cement floor, he saw something in his father he'd never seen before—a frail human being.

"You sure you're okay?"

Jonah managed a half smile. "I'm fine, son. Thanks."

"What happened?"

He sighed. "I saw you run out of the press conference this morning and hoped we could talk before tonight. Albright told me your GPS had been spotted on the golf course. I presumed you were simply walking around the property, thinking and probably needing your privacy, so I came alone. I haven't had a personal bodyguard in years. Not since I built the cabin. I just never expected to be ambushed on my own golf course by a young man brandishing a semiautomatic. Foolish of me, I realize."

Foolish, maybe. But also far more considerate than Mark would have expected. Another sign that his father had changed. "Don't beat yourself up. I'm just glad you're okay."

Their kidnappers hadn't even bothered tying them. They'd just kept their random arsenal of weapons pointed at his dad's throat long enough to realize no one could fit through the skylight. Then they'd locked them in and left. From what he could tell, they hadn't even left anyone guarding the door. That worried him. Al and his boys had been in a hurry to leave.

For a moment, when the door had opened, he'd considered just barreling through them—trusting that a bunch of jumpy, badly armed, drug-addled teenagers probably wouldn't hit what they were aiming at. But that would have put his father's life in further danger. Not to mention the teenagers themselves.

Maybe it was odd to be wanting to save the very people putting his own life at risk. But he'd seen too many broken, hurting young people like that in battlefields the world over. At least if they were arrested here they'd be able to get the help they needed behind bars. Maybe some of them would even get a chance at a better way of life.

"I've been following your company." Jonah's words broke in through his son's distracted thoughts. "You do good work, and some of your solutions have been pretty inventive. I am sorry I tried to stop you. That was wrong of me—arrogant and shortsighted."

He ran his hand through his gray hair, mirroring the gesture Mark himself had done a thousand times before when faced with a seemingly impossible problem. "I hope you and your sister can settle matters amicably. It would be nice to think work like yours could be part of the Shields legacy."

Words of protest and argument sprang to Mark's mind. This was not the right time for this conversation—and hardly the right place. But even as the words of anger and frustration echoed back within the recesses of his heart, he could hear another stronger, calmer voice reminding him it was not his job to decide the timing—only the response.

"What happened to you?" Mark asked. "For my whole life, you were so devoted to building up the almighty Shields Corp that half the time I didn't even know what city you were in."

But the words stuck in his throat as he turned and saw the broken look on his father's face. This was no longer a defiant man hiding behind his office walls. This was one who had finally stepped out into the desolation he'd unwittingly left behind.

Mark shook his head. No, he didn't need to know how it had happened. He could see his father's mind formulating a defense. But Mark held up a hand. The Lord knew his family was desperate for a cease-fire. Maybe he could be the first to lay down his arms.

"It's okay," Mark said. "Just tell me why on earth did you give up your company?"

"The last thing your grandmother ever told me was that she thought I'd lost my way." Jonah looked down. "I'd sacrificed my family and shut out God. She made me promise to try building something—anything—with my own two hands again. Asked me to pray, to humble myself before God again. It took time for her words to sink in. Longer still for my heart to change. But as it did, slowly the company changed around me. If I don't make it out of here alive, please tell your sister—" He swallowed hard.

"You are going be able to tell her yourself." Mark stood. "I'm going to find us a way out of here. Hopefully one of these cleaning solutions will have the right chemical components to blow the lock off the door. If we can make a big enough explosion, it should disable anyone who might still be outside the door. The shelves aren't much, but if we take them apart, they'll give us a fighting chance. Do you have anything in your pockets that might help?"

His father patted down his work clothes. "How about half a book of matches, a battery and a couple of nails?"

Mark grinned. "Perfect."

It wasn't exactly easy to think with a gun pressed against her temple.

"Talk me through it again." The gun rattled in

Billy's hand. "How do you set up a broadcast?" His emaciated form was hidden in an oversized sweatshirt. Sweat dripped down his face.

She closed her eyes. "Why are you doing this? Do you even know?"

Maybe it wasn't wise to talk back to someone holding a gun to her head. But now that she was finally looking directly into the sunken, hollow eyes of the very young man who had chased, attacked, threatened and terrorized her ever since she'd stepped onto the platform in Cobalt, all she could see was a boy who was not only capable of cruelty and violence but who was also very, very afraid.

"You didn't sign up for any of this, did you?" she ventured. "Someone just offered you money or drugs to follow me up from Toronto and make sure I didn't go off course? After all, fifty thousand dollars is a lot to risk on just a GPS tracker. If I'd gotten off at an unexpected stop or lost my phone, there goes your payday. Did you know the rockslide on the train tracks wasn't an accident? That someone wanted the train to stop in Cobalt?"

His eyebrows rose. She'd take that as a no.

"Let me guess. Al told you all you had to do was help him get me to the van. Easy money. But then I ran, and you were forced to chase me. Then what? You were told you wouldn't get your money until I was caught?"

"Stop it," he said. "Just show me how to work the machine."

"It just kept evolving, didn't it? Spying on where I'd went, taking my pictures to send to…who? The person who'd hired Al? Maybe to prove you hadn't lost me completely?"

He looked down.

"Blocking the road, kidnapping two people instead of one, bringing more people in… It all just kept spiraling out of control, didn't it? You still weren't getting paid."

"I said stop it!" he shouted. "Look! I can hurt you, all right! We get the money for turning you over. They don't care what we do to you first."

"Who?"

A noise like thunder exploded above their heads. The room shook. Plaster fell from the ceiling. Billy screamed.

NINETEEN

Mark eased himself up off the floor and glanced out through the wreckage of the storage room door. The small explosive had been crude but effective. He peered through the smoke. The hallway was deserted. He braced a length of shelving over his shoulder like a baseball bat and handed another to his father as a shield. "Come on, Dad. Let's go."

The two men had barely reached the bottom of the stairs when Katie rounded the corner. Mark caught her with one arm, pulling her into his side.

"I thought I told you to run."

"Billy had me at gunpoint. Then he freaked out and ran away."

"He did what?"

"There was an explosion—"

"That was me. I blew open the door—"

"One second Billy had a gun to my throat and was trying to get me to show him how to set up a radio broadcast. The next, he was screaming like the roof was going to cave in. He slammed the case shut and ran."

"What?" Sure, their kidnappers probably hadn't expected the storage door to blow open. But he'd figured they'd have been running toward the sound, not away.

They heard an engine turn over. He sprinted for the doorway, just in time to see the last of Al's teenagers leaping into the back of a van. Then it took off down the road before they'd even gotten the back door closed.

It seemed their kidnappers had given up on holding them all and had narrowed their prisoners down to just one—Katie's boss. Now they might be his only chance to make it out alive. They had to save him.

"Dad. Are there any vehicles here?"

"There are golf carts."

It wasn't ideal, but it would have to do.

"Can you drive?" Mark called to Katie as they chased the old man around to the side of the house.

"Well enough."

"Okay, then. Then keep your head down and try not to get shot." He looked at his dad, who was already climbing into the nearest cart. "That goes for you, too."

Katie grit her teeth and focused on keeping the golf cart on the narrow, winding road. There was no way they'd be able to catch up with the van once it reached the open road. But as long as they were weaving around potholes on an unpaved road, there was still a chance. Jonah hunched low in the backseat, trying to get through to security on the ham radio. She could see the back of the van now, its back door flying open again as it spun around a corner.

"What do you want to do?" she shouted to Mark.

"We've got to slow them down before they reach the highway." He stood up in the passenger seat. "If they manage to get into that maze of rural roads that run around here, the police might not find them until it's too late."

Which could mean Ethan being killed or tortured. As much as she disliked her boss, she knew what it was like to be the one tied up and terrified in the back of a van. If they could distract the driver to slow the van by even a few minutes, it could give the police time to catch up.

A flurry of bullets shot out of the back of the van now, spraying high through the air before landing ineffectually on the road ahead of them. Then the van turned another corner, the momentum throwing the door shut again.

"Tell me the windshield is bulletproof," he said, turning back toward his father.

But Jonah was talking into the radio now and didn't seem to hear him.

Okay, so hopefully that meant a whole phalanx of police and security were heading their way.

Grabbing the roof with one hand and a golf club with the other, Mark pulled himself up to standing. He braced himself against the dashboard. "Can you get alongside them?"

"I can try." She nudged the golf cart forward until they were skimming along the roadside parallel to the van. Just like the vehicle Al had thrown them in yesterday, this one had no windows in the back, which meant they were probably going to be a whole lot safer beside them than behind them, unless someone was suicidal enough to try shooting out the driver's window.

Mark leaned out the side of the golf cart. She caught a glimpse of Billy's face behind the wheel. The teen's eyes opened wide. Mark swung the golf club hard, taking out the driver's side window. The van swerved toward the tree line. Mark grabbed the dashboard with both hands. Katie hit the brakes. The van slammed into a tree with such force she was afraid for its passengers.

The driver's door opened, and the ashen-faced teenager tumbled out. Then the van's back door swung open, showing a tangled mass of bodies and weapons as the boys struggled to their feet. Al and Ethan were nowhere to be seen.

Mark leaped from the cart, the club still poised over his shoulder. But before a prayer could even form on her lips, she heard the screech of tires. She looked up. A black SUV and two police cars had pulled up in front of them. Within moments, police had the van surrounded.

The SUV door opened, and Sunny stepped out. "I don't know what kind of stunt you're pulling here, but it's not going to work."

The gentle strains of pleasant conversation and a string quartet floated through the night air. Mark crossed through the courtyard to Katie's guest townhouse, weaving through the well-dressed crowd. Soft white lights twinkled in the branches of the trees. Frustration burned inside his heart.

His sister had gone ahead with the party. All of Al's ragtag army had been arrested without incident. But Al and Ethan hadn't been in the van. Neither was the broadcast unit. Billy said Al had taken it.

Thanks to Billy's cooperation, the ringleader had now been identified as Allan Blau. The small-time drug and weapons dealer had a history of mental illness. He'd operated out of Langtry Glen before the building's demolition had forced him to find a new client base. Police now presumed he was behind over a dozen death threats that had been sent to the Shieldses in the weeks that followed.

Billy had been pressed into helping him kidnap Katie in exchange for having a sizable drug debt erased. Yes, he knew Al had been able to track her cell phone by GPS, but he didn't know how the tracker had gotten into her phone. He didn't know who had offered to pay Al for her capture—if such a person even existed—or have any idea where Al had taken Ethan and the broadcast unit.

Mark shuddered. The power of one delusional man to destroy the life of others was terrifying. Now the police were combing the surrounding area for Ethan. His father was resting, safe in his home with a security guard at the door and Albright by his side. Yet somewhere, lost in the partying crowd, his sister was eating and mingling as though nothing had happened. She hadn't even been willing to talk to him. He straightened his tie. Albright had taken the liberty of having someone drop off a selection of business attire and formal wear in his room. It was the first time he'd been back in a suit since he'd left his world. But when he'd looked out the window of his guest room and seen the overdressed crowd below, it had seemed more respectful to change into something more formal before walking through the complex to Katie's suite. As much as he disapproved of Sunny's actions, he wasn't going to embarrass her or make a scene by being spotted by some reporter sauntering through a gala in muddy jeans. Besides, whoever had selected his wardrobe hadn't thought to include anything casual.

He glanced up to the sky.

Oh, Lord, how could his own sister go on with

a party when a man's life was in danger? How had his sister's priorities gotten so messed up? Was there anything he could do to make things right again?

Then he saw Katie, standing on the balcony of her townhouse. Her hair was pulled back off her face. Pale blue silk fell from her shoulders down to her knees. His breath caught in his throat. She was beautiful.

Her eyes met his. She smiled. He watched as she tilted her head and had a quiet word with the security guard standing beside her. Then she started down the stairs toward him. But suddenly, he was rushing up the stairs toward her, reaching her before she'd even made it halfway, catching her around the waist, pulling her into his arms. His lips brushed over her cheek until he found her mouth, allowing himself to kiss her for barely a moment before pulling back again.

"I hope this is okay," she said, glancing down at her clothes. "It doesn't really feel like attending the party is the right thing to do. But—"

"You are the most beautiful sight I've ever seen."

She sighed happily. "The police had finished questioning me. I had an interesting conversation with work. Then, I saw the party had started."

"Yeah. I don't know what Sunny was thinking." Taking her hand, he led her down the stairs to the courtyard below. "Do you want to tell me how things went with work?"

"In a bit. How is your dad?"

"Tired. He still feels foolish for heading to the clubhouse without backup. But he's okay. His cardiologist just wants to keep an eye on him." His arm slid around her waist. Her head fell against his shoulder. Within moments, they were lost together in a sea of gowns and suits. Waiters waved trays of sparkling drinks and hors d'oeuvres in their direction. Security guards nodded as they passed. He tightened his arm around her.

Mark glanced up at the canopy of stars spreading out above their heads. This moment was almost perfect. They were together, safe, alone. And yet he couldn't let himself enjoy it. Her boss's life was still at risk. The man responsible was still lurking out there, somewhere in the darkness. There were so many questions still unanswered.

Not to mention the fact that in barely more than a day's time, he'd be climbing onto an airplane, jetting off to the other side of the world, leaving her behind. Would she be willing to wait for him? Was that even fair of him to ask?

"Are you okay?" Her voice brushed against his ear.

"No." He stopped walking and turned her toward him. "Believe me, I want to be. I want to just let myself be here in this moment with you but I can't. I wish I could say that knowing you're safe is enough for me. But it's not. I need to know that horrible man you work for is going to make it home safe. I need to know Al will never recruit another kid, get one more person hooked on drugs or hurt anyone else for the rest of his miserable life. I need to know that I'll be able to work something out with my sister and my father, and save TRUST—"

Her fingers ran up his arms and onto his shoulders. "You need to know you did everything you could. Not just to save me but everyone."

He nodded. "Is that wrong of me? Does it make me sound ungrateful?"

She laughed and shook her head lightly. "No." Her lips brushed against his cheek. "That makes you rather wonderful."

"Well, if it isn't my long-lost brother!" Sunny was striding through the crowd toward them. Her dark hair was piled high above her head like a crown. A sneer curled her red lips. "That was a pretty neat stunt you pulled, getting Dad alone like that."

Voices stopped. Eyes turned toward them.

"What stunt?" Mark kept his voice low. "We were kidnapped. Our lives were threatened." The hint of a growl slipped through his measured words. "Have you even gone to see him since we escaped? He was pretty shaken up."

She sniffed.

"Come on. This has got to stop." His voice softened. "I know Dad has made a lot of mistakes. But so have we." Mark stepped forward and reached out for his sister's arm. "Please, Sun. Let's go talk somewhere private."

She jumped back as though he had stung her. "Why?" She spun her arms around in a circle at the crowd. "Because you're embarrassed by me? Embarrassed of this family?"

"No," Mark started. Then he caught himself. *Lord, give me the strength to be honest.* "Okay, yes. I was ashamed of Shields Corp and everything our family name had come to mean. But not of you. Never of you." He shook his head. "You are my little sister. I love you."

"You left me!" Sudden tears built in her eyes. "You ran away. First our mother left. Then you. Then our grandmother." She ran her fingers over her eyes. "I was left with nothing but a father who was going through some kind of late life spiritual crisis and a company he no longer felt like running. So, you know what I did? I stepped up. I worked hard at becoming the perfect little daughter. Working twelve hours a day, seven days a week, never taking a vacation, never having a party, never doing anything but trying to prove to him—to everyone—that I could do it. That I could run this company without the help of anyone."

"I know, and he's proud of you. I'm proud of you." Again, he stretched out his arms toward his little sister, and for a moment, he thought she was going to let him hug her.

But then her arms snapped over her chest. "Then look at how he repays me. He turns around and gives half of everything to you. Even though you don't deserve it. Because, he says, we're equal in his eyes. Because no matter where you go, or what you do, he loves you."

"He loves you, too, Sun. He's just not very good at showing it. I think he's trying to make up for lost time the only way he knows how before it's too late."

Her eyes flashed. "I'm still going to sue you for what's rightfully mine."

Sadness broke over him like a wave. *Dear Lord, how had everything gotten so broken? What can I possibly do to fix it?* "I hope you change your mind, because, yeah, I could use the money to do so much good. But that doesn't matter to me anywhere near as much as you do. I love you, Sun. Not the money. Not this place. And I would give it up if it meant not losing you."

She looked up through lids heavy with tears.

"I'm sorry I was not as good a brother to you as I should've been. I was so busy trying to do what I thought was right that I didn't stop to realize how it was hurting you. Please, forgive me. Please, come with me overseas and see the kind of work I'm doing. I want you to be part of my life."

Her mouth opened, and for a moment, hope leaped in his heart. But then the same hard look spread over her face again. "It's too late."

Mark watched as she strode away. The crowd filled in around her.

"You did the right thing." Katie touched his arm. "She just needs some time to calm down."

He blew out a hard breath. He needed out of this crowd and away from the noise and the chaos. He needed to be somewhere he could think. "You okay if we get out of here?"

She nodded.

Mark led her away from the crowd and pulled a compact but powerful walkie-talkie off his belt. "Albright?"

"Yes, si—Mark," Albright's voice crackled back.

"Do we still have any boats on the lake?"

"I'm afraid just a fishing boat. Your father sold the power boats."

"That's fine." Something small and peaceful would be perfect. "Please inform security I'm going to take Katie out on the lake."

The oars cut cleanly into the water. He hadn't even tried to fire up the small outboard motor, preferring instead to lean his shoulders into it and let his muscles do the work. Katie sat curled up in the prow of the boat, her fingers trailing idly through the water. The noise of the party faded into the distance, replaced by the gentle creak of the oars turning against the side of the boat and dipping in and out of the water.

He took a deep breath and let it out again. Here, he could breathe.

"That there is my own tiny part of the world." He pointed to where the shadow of a small island rose from the center of the lake. "I learned to swim there. Zack and I used to hike through the forest to the closest point of the shore and then swim out and back. Hadn't even realized it technically belonged to my grandmother until she left it to me in her will. I used to say I was going to build my own home there."

"Like your father."

"Yeah…" The oars dipped down and up again. Was he really so different from his father? Sure, he'd given his life to helping others instead of making money. But below the surface, were their lives really so different? The long hours? The punishing schedule? Pushing everyone else away because the business he'd created demanded everything from him?

He'd judged his father harshly for not knowing how to fit a wife and children into his life. But was he really that much more able to make room in his life for Katie? When he'd left all this and changed his name, "Mark Armor" and "Jonah Shields Junior" had felt like two different people. But were they really?

"They offered me Ethan's job." Katie's voice cut through his thoughts. "On an interim basis, at least initially. They want me back in Toronto first thing tomorrow morning. Doesn't matter that it's Sunday. The board is opening the offices to develop a full media strategy on how we're going to handle Ethan's kidnapping."

He paused rowing for a moment, letting the small boat drift. "Are congratulations in order?"

"I turned them down." Her fingers swirled through the water, as if composing music in her mind. "I asked for a leave of absence. They agreed to two weeks' medical leave, though after that I can dip into my holiday time. I have plenty saved."

He went back to rowing. "I thought you were dying to take over the editor's desk."

"I was. Dying. But over the past few days I realized how much I missed living." She shrugged. "So I'm going to try taking some time just to think. And pray. And sleep. Maybe read a book or go for a walk. Figure out where I'm really going and why."

He nodded. Something told him he'd be doing a whole lot of thinking on that flight to Lebanon on Monday.

The small boat followed the curve of the lake around toward the clubhouse. A bright light shone from the front window. Funny, he thought the police had already cleared the place. He reached for the walkie-talkie. "Albright?"

"Yeah? Mark?"

"Is there supposed to be anyone in the clubhouse?"

There was a pause. "I believe security has some-

one watching the road in and out. I think they finished with the building."

"Well, there's someone there now. Maybe you
should get them to send—"

A sudden burst of static broke over the line. The
signal screeched. Then a new voice took over the air-
waves. "Help! Somebody! Anybody! They're going
to kill me!"

Katie gasped. "Ethan!"

The channel faded to static again. Mark searched
through the channels but couldn't reach either Albright or Ethan. Chances were the radio transmitter
was trying to broadcast on all channels again. He
started the engine. Did this mean Ethan had somehow escaped with the broadcast unit? Or did Al
have him locked up and Ethan had tried to use the
unit to call for help?

He glanced up at the bright light shining in the
clubhouse window. At least now they knew where
he was.

Mark cut the engine as they came upon the bank.
The light had disappeared from the window even
before they reached shore. He dug out a flashlight
out from under the seat. "Keep trying the walkie-
talkie, and see if you can reach Albright. I'm hoping
he got the message and is sending a whole team of
security heading out this way, but I can't be sure."

He pulled a rope from the bottom of the boat,

climbed out and tethered it to the dock. Katie scrambled out after him.

"No, we'll be safer staying together."

He opened his mouth and then shut it again. If the past few days had taught him anything, it was that sometimes it helped to have a partner. "Okay then. Just stay back if I tell you to. Don't be a hero."

"You got it."

He grinned. He was going to have to figure out a way to marry her when this was all over.

The windows were dark. The clubhouse looked just as deserted as it had when they'd fled it with his father only a few hours earlier. The huge front door slid open smoothly. Their feet echoed in the empty entranceway. Mark crossed the room and waved for her to follow him down the hallway. "Now, I think I saw the light coming from the—" The words froze in his throat, and his hands rose slowly in the air. He backed into the room, followed by Al and the long, angular barrel of an assault rifle.

TWENTY

"Down on the floor." Al gripped the assault rifle like a sniper. "Now."

Mark was stock-still. He dropped the flashlight and held his hands out in front of him like boxer's gloves. "You've lost your army. All those boys you coerced into helping you have been arrested and police know exactly who you are." He calmly stepped toward Al with a confidence that made Katie's breath catch in her throat. "You're nothing but a sick two-bit drug dealer with delusions of grandeur, who probably doesn't even know now to work that AK-47."

"I was there the day your family destroyed my home." Al tightened his grasp. "Someone pushed a button, and then there was nothing left but rubble. Now I'm going to do the same to yours."

"You're the one destroying lives." Mark took another step toward the barrel pointed between his eyes. "I'm not going to let you destroy any more. This is my family's home and your last warning."

Al leveled Mark in his sights. Mark dove through

the air toward him, just as the gun exploded upward. A loud spray of bullets tore up the ceiling as
the force kicked Al off balance.

Mark caught him hard in the stomach and knocked
the gun from his hands. He swung low and brought
his arm up to the other man's chest, pushing him
back toward the ground. But Al rolled over quickly
and lunged at his throat.

Katie ran for the gun and yanked out the magazine
before throwing it out into the dense underbrush.
Then she turned back, only to watch desperately as
the two men rolled on the ground in a mess of fists
and feet and flailing limbs, struggling for domi-
nance. Within seconds, Mark had thrown Al against
the floor again, and for a moment she thought he
had him pinned. But with one desperate lunge, Al
head-butted Mark hard in the face. Mark's grasp
slackened. The drug dealer squirmed free and ran
out the front of the building.

Katie rushed to Mark's side. "You okay?"

"Yeah. Like I told you, there's nothing more stupid
than a novice with an AK-47. Fool things always…"

"Pull up and to the right, I remember."

Mark grinned. He leaped to his feet. "Go. Find
Ethan. I'm not letting Al get away this time."

Desperately, she searched the first floor, shining the flashlight over every corner, calling Ethan's
name as she went. The dining room was empty. So

was the kitchen. She reached the lounge and opened the door.

"Oh, Katie!" A figure rose from the armchair and bowed at her like a shaky marionette. "You're exactly the person I was hoping to see. So, tell me, how is the story going so far? Is it all over the news?" He was still drunk and probably high. But at least he was still alive. Thank God. By the look of it, Al hadn't even touched him.

"I heard your distress signal—"

"Oh, you heard that!" He beamed a wide, wobbly and disconcerting smile, as though he expected applause. "I thought it would add to the story. Al was playing with the radio anyway. But he didn't like me touching things and sent me downstairs."

"Downstairs? What were you doing upstairs?"

He waved a hand, like he was swatting her question away. "Now, the first thing I need you to do is get the power back on and fire up an internet connection. I really want to end this story with a bang."

She stretched out her hand. "Just come with me now, and you can use the internet back in your room."

He dropped back into the armchair and crossed his arms. "I'm not going anywhere."

She sighed. No wonder Al hadn't bothered tying him up. He'd probably just supplied him with so many illegal substances that he didn't know he was in danger.

"Ethan," she said gently, as if coaxing a very small child out of a tree, "you've been kidnapped—"

"No, I haven't."

"Yes, you have. We were in a helicopter, and it crashed. Then some people took us hostage."

He scowled. "I know, I know." He shook his head. "The story was all getting really exciting, too, and then everyone stopped doing what I told them...."

"No, Ethan. This isn't a story. It's real. You're in the clubhouse on the Shields estate—"

"I know!" He stormed over to the desk, snatched up a lamp and threw it against the wall. It smashed. "But Al won't let me go until I come up with the fifty thousand dollars I promised him!"

Al scrambled into a golf cart and started the engine. Mark pushed his body to run faster, forcing his way through a wall of physical pain even as it screamed in his head like a fury. The golf cart lurched forward, stalled, then sped forward again. But in an instant, Mark had reached it.

He leaped up onto the side and grabbed Al around the neck. Al's fist flew hard into his face, filling his vision with stars. But throwing his weight backward, he yanked Al from his seat. For a second, he could see the terror in his eyes as they fell through the air. They hit the ground, and Mark lost his grip. There was a screech and then a loud metallic bang as the golf cart plowed into a tree.

He leaped to his feet just in time to see Al pulling a knife from his boot. "Just let me walk out of here, and no one needs to get hurt."

Mark nearly laughed. "I can't do that. You terrorized the woman I love. You came into my family home and threatened my father. You think that knife is going to protect you from me?"

Mark threw himself at Al just as the weapon flashed through the air. Grabbing his arm, Mark forced him down to the ground. He smacked Al's wrist backward into the dirt until the weapon fell from his hand.

"Stand up." He grabbed Al by the collar and pulled him up to face him. "I don't want to hurt you. So you're going to show me where you're keeping Ethan. Then you're going to sit nice and quietly while we wait for the police."

"Please." Al shook his head, writhing in panic like a drowning man. "You have to let me go."

"Look, I will drag you in if I have to—"

"The building's going to explode."

"Like I was ever really going to pay him!" Ethan spluttered. "I mean, who'd really pay fifty thousand dollars for you?"

His words struck Katie in the chest like bullets. "You did this?" She stumbled back. "You hired some random criminal to terrorize me for a story?"

"Al's my guy." He crossed his arms in front of his

chest. "He finds me things when I need them, and I pay him for it."

"Like drugs?" She glanced toward the door. Where was Mark?

"And my gun and sometimes women. He knows how to get me stuff." He sniffed. "None of this is my fault. The board said they'd fire me if we didn't get subscriptions up, and none of you could get me a decent story. So I told Al to find me a really good shocking story, like a kidnapping. He suggested kidnapping me. But I thought it would be good if we got some ransom pictures, and we wanted whoever it was to look really scared. Like they thought they were going to die. Add some tension to it. Plus I was hardly going to get credit for the story if I wasn't in the office running the paper. Besides, we figured the longer it lasted, the more papers we'd sell, and it's not like I wanted to be locked in some closet for a week. I've got a life. So we decided he'd just grab one of the women who work for me."

Her hand rose to her throat. "You paid your dealer to hurt me?"

"Kidnap. He was only supposed to kidnap you." He rolled his eyes. "This mess is all your fault, you know. If you'd just let them kidnap you already, we'd have a big, wonderful exclusive in the paper about how one of our staff was…I don't know…kidnapped by some crazy person. But you had to pick this week to be difficult."

Is that why he'd picked her? Because he thought she wouldn't fight back? Is that where all her compliance had gotten her? "You bugged my phone. You sent me north to the middle of nowhere because you wanted me isolated, vulnerable…"

"You think it was too much?" he said. "Tying it into the Shields thing? It was Al's idea. He really hates the Shieldses. Like, obsessively. He insisted on this specific story assignment. He was going to grab you in Kapuskasing and use you to break into the Shields party somehow… I don't know…. I wasn't listening. As long as I got my kidnap story, I was leaving the details up to him.

"But Al got kind of sidetracked. He was on his way up here and saw someone he thought looked like Shields Junior at a gas station, so he followed him to a farmhouse in Cobalt. Next thing I know he's saying he's going to make the train stop in Cobalt and kidnap you there, so he can try to grab your friend, too. I said I didn't care as long as he kidnapped you. But it was probably more than he could handle. I just thought, hey, people hate Shields, you know? Hit two juicy birds with one stone and then tie them both together with a big, fat bow." He grinned. "It was really cool when he managed to get me pictures. I'm thinking a photo spread."

An almost hysterical giggle was building in the back of her throat. He'd actually thought he could bribe his drug dealer to kidnap her as a stunt to sell papers. This was the Ethan who scared her. The drug-addled narcissist who showed up at work dead-eyed, then carried on an hour-long conversation with an empty chair, and because they'd all been so afraid of getting fired, they let him get away with it. The overindulged playboy who no one had ever said no to. No wonder he thought he could get away with blowing something up or kidnapping someone as a means to propel his little publication to the big time—he'd been too pampered, drugged and indulged to ever realize the world held any limits.

"Ethan! This is serious. People have been hurt. We could've been killed. The helicopter pilot died. Not to mention whoever was in the van when it exploded—"

A dangerous scowl flickered across his face. "That van had nothing to do with me. I didn't order bombs. It's not my fault Al improvised. Did you know he actually demanded I come up here this morning? He even made me bring up a bag for him."

"What was in the bag?"

"I dunno. Some kind of bomb. I left it under a table in the party tent. He said it would add to the story if we blew some things up."

"Like a gala full of people?" No wonder Billy and the other teenagers had run screaming when they heard Mark blow the storage door open. Al had them playing with explosives.

"I think a couple of the guys set some up in other

places around the complex, too," he said. "He didn't tell me all the locations. I just know he got all hyped up about it when he knew we had a radio detonator."

Radio detonator…Mark's broadcast unit. Katie's mind was reeling so fast she could hardly put words to her thoughts. "Ethan. Focus. Is Al going to use Mark's radio unit to set off the other bombs?"

"I guess." His shoulders rose and fell limply. "It's not fair. He was playing with it, but he took it away."

"And you said it's upstairs?"

Another shrug.

She grabbed his arm. "Ethan. Listen to me. You've got to get out of here, and I've got to find Mark. This is not your story anymore, and Al's just using you. You're not the boss here. You're just another stupid junkie to him. We have to go to the police. Now—"

He lunged before she could react, grabbing her by the shoulders, pushing her into the wall. A small gun flashed in his hand. "I am your boss." He pressed it to her temple. "And you will obey me."

TWENTY-ONE

Ethan's hand clenched her throat. The other forced the tip of the gun into her skin. "You work for me. I own you—just like Al—and I am going to direct exactly how this is going to go. First, you're going to help me get Al arrested, so I don't have to pay him. Then you are going to tell the world that I'm your hero and I rescued you—"

She could feel the paralyzing grip of fear creeping up her throat. But she gulped a deep breath and forced it back. "No, Ethan. I won't."

He dropped his grip on her and swung. His fist flew through the air, hitting her across the face, snapping her jaw sideways so violently her neck screamed in pain. A wave of nausea swept over her. Her legs gave way.

"You work for me," he screamed. "You belong to me. You must obey me."

"No. I will never belong to you."

"Then you can die for all I care." He threw himself onto her back, forcing her face into the ground.

Oh, God. Please don't abandon me now... You hem me in behind and before. You lay your hand upon me. She screamed with every ounce of air left in her lungs and swung backward at him, her fists falling ineffectually against his sides.

He laughed. "Give it up, Katie. You're on your own now. You are all mine." He grabbed a fistful of hair and yanked her head back so hard pain blinded her vision. Her hands shot out, reaching for anything she could grab on to.

Even the darkness will not be dark to you... For darkness is as light to you... Her fingers brushed against the remains of the broken lamp. She grasped the base and swung it back hard toward him. A satisfying crack filled the room as her weapon made contact. Ethan grunted and fell off her. She pulled herself onto her hands and knees, gasping for breath.

"Katie!" Mark appeared in the doorway. "You okay?"

She coughed. Then nodded. "Where's Al?"

"I let him run."

He crossed the room and reached for her hand. "Come on. We've got to get out of here. This whole place is going to explode."

She shook her head. "We can't. They planted bombs at the gala. Al set up your suitcase studio as the remote detonator."

His face turned the color of ash. "Where?" He

grabbed Ethan and rolled him over. The editor moaned faintly, but his eyes didn't open.

"It's upstairs." She dragged herself to her feet. "He's got a gun."

Mark patted him down quickly. "Can't find it and we don't have time to go searching for it." He turned to face her. His hands slid onto her shoulders. "Do what you can to get him out of here. But if he won't go, just leave him. I need you to get as far away from here as you can. Al said there was a bomb in this building, as well. But if the remote detonator for the other bombs is also here, then this building will have to be the last one set to explode. Otherwise, it would just blow up the radio detonator itself before it could set the other bombs off. I just don't know how much time that will give us." He kissed her cheek, dropped her shoulders and turned to go.

"No." Her hand grabbed his. "I'm going with you. I know where I belong and it's not abandoning you to save myself. If this building explodes, who knows how big the blast radius is going to be or even if I'll be able to get far enough away. If I've only got a few minutes left on this earth, I know where I want to be."

"Okay." He swallowed hard. "Let's go do this."

They ran into the hallway and for the stairs. The stench of gasoline and motor oil floated down toward them. Mark squeezed her hand, then stopped and beckoned her to step behind him. He glanced through the broken door. The radio unit was humming on the middle of the floor. Buckets lined what remained of the shelves around it. "Fertilizer bomb, I'm guessing," he said. "Smells like one anyway. Probably a mixture of gasoline, motor oil and good old ammonium nitrate."

"Can you disable the bomb?"

"Hardly, I wouldn't know where to start, and I wouldn't want to try. But if there's one thing I know how to do it's how to stop the unit from sending a signal." Mark slid his feet cautiously across the floor as though it was a layer of razor-thin ice. "Whatever you do, don't touch anything. Don't even breathe if you can help it."

Intuitively, his fingers ran across the keyboard, and the unit sprang to life. "Now, come on, baby," he whispered under his breath, typing in his password. "Show me what they did to you."

Invalid password. He groaned and tried the default password.

Invalid password. "Fine, if you want to play it that way…"

"You locked out?"

"They changed the passwords, yeah." His fingers flew over the keyboard like a storm. "But don't worry. I built in a back door. What can you tell me about the buckets?"

"There are six of them, and they have wires."

Screens filled with ASCII text popped up in front of him. "You see a timer?"

"There's half a cell phone."

"Don't touch it. A bomb has got to have a detonator. Otherwise no bomb-maker would ever make it out alive. So either you set a timer that automatically trips the switch when it goes off...or...you..." The main menu popped up on the screen. "Or you set it off with some kind of remote signal."

He'd made it to the broadcast scheduling screen. There were three pending radio broadcasts—all set moments apart. The first was scheduled to start in less than five minutes. "Like a radio signal." He spun the laptop around to face her. "We've got five minutes before things start exploding. The good news is that the lovely bomb in the corner is probably not supposed to detonate until the unit is done setting off the other ones."

"And how long does that give us to get out of here?"

"About eight minutes."

"Well, get on with it then."

Mark grinned. Now all he had to do was shut down the signals. It should just be as simple as opening the schedule and canceling...

Up came a warning box: *You do not have authorization to delete or modify these broadcasts.*

"Can't you just turn it off?"

"No." He sighed. "We set it up with a backup

timer system so the transmitter would come on automatically whenever a broadcast was scheduled even if the power was off. I can't disable that from here." The transmitter was integrated, too. There was no way he could disable it without breaking the entire unit open. He pounded in the DOS in vain, trying to open the device manager.

"How long have we got?"

"Seven minutes."

A second warning box jumped onto the screen. *You do not have authorization to modify device function.* He groaned and ran his hand through his sweat-soaked hair. The one time he wanted the unit to fail it was running exactly the way he'd designed it to. If he could only get it to crash like it had when he'd shown Katie the default emergency broadcasts—

"Tsunami!"

"What?"

"Get back downstairs and get ready to run when you hear me coming. I can't stop this place from blowing up—but I can stop the other bombs." Mark let his fingers flow over the keys, shutting his mind to the warning beeps as he hit permissions' block after permissions' block, until finally the screen filled with the list of emergency broadcasts.

He scrolled down and hit the key for Tsunami. A series of sound waves popped up on the screen. He hit Play and eased his way back across the floor as the sequence of eight long beeps played. The machine froze. The screen went black.

He nearly laughed out loud. "I got it!" He ran for the stairs. "Katie! I managed to stop the—"

Then he heard her screaming. He sprinted down the hallway as Katie's cries for help echoed around him. She wasn't in the lobby. Or the dining room. Then he heard a crash from the direction of the lounge.

He rounded the corner in time to see Ethan yanking her by the hair, pulling her backward into the stairway.

"Let her go!" He barreled toward them.

Ethan glanced up toward him, only for a second, but it was enough for Katie. Swinging her arm back, she elbowed him hard in the gut. He grunted and let go. She ran forward, but within seconds, Ethan had jumped on her again, throwing her hard against the floor. "You...can...not...leave...me..."

Mark grabbed Ethan by the shirt and yanked him upward. Ethan squirmed. His eyes darted back and forth wildly. His pupils almost completely engulfed his eyes in a sea of black. The man was so high Mark wouldn't be surprised if he was hallucinating now.

"We've got to get out of here." Mark shook him by his shoulders.

Ethan spat in his face. "I'm not going anywhere—"

They didn't have time for this. Mark caught Katie's eye. She nodded. He decked Ethan in the jaw. Her boss crumpled to the floor like a rag doll. Mark hauled up Ethan's limp body and slung it over one shoulder. "I don't know how big the blast radius is going to be. Our best bet is to get back to the boat and try to put as much distance as we can between us and the explosion."

Katie slid her arm under Ethan's other shoulder.

"Go," Mark shouted. "I've got him."

"I told you we're in this together. I'm not leaving without you."

"Have I told you I love you?"

Katie grinned. Then he saw her grit her teeth. They ran, dragging Ethan's limp body between them. The cement was rough. Trees pressed up against the path, threatening to pull Ethan's body from their grasp. Ethan began to groan.

"I've got him. Untie the boat." He dragged Ethan into the boat and dropped him on the floor. She untied them from the dock and scrambled in. Then she reached under the seats, grabbed a paddle and pushed the boat away from shore. Mark pulled on the engine cord. Nothing. He yanked again. It coughed and sputtered, then stopped. He yanked the cord again. He'd flood the engine if he wasn't careful.

Ethan swore. "No, no, no." He stumbled to his feet. "The story can't end like this. I have to go back and be the hero."

The tiny boat bumped against a rock. Katie nudged the boat toward the middle of the lake.

"Take me back, or I will blow your head off!" Too late they saw the handgun in Ethan's hand. Narrowing him in his sights, he pointed the gun at Mark's head.

Mark raised his hands. "Listen to me. There is a bomb in the clubhouse. Any second now there's going to be nothing left but a fireball and a pile of ashes."

Ethan clicked the safety off. His finger reached for the trigger. Katie swung the paddle through the air like a baseball bat. The wood caught Ethan hard across the shoulders. The boat rocked violently. He pitched sideways and fell over the side of the boat into the lake.

"Drop the gun and get back in the boat, Ethan!" she shouted.

"I lost it!" He swore, thrashing around in the waist-deep water. "Where'd it go?"

"Forget the gun." She stretched her hand toward him. "Grab my hand, and we'll pull you in."

"I'm the hero. I need to be here when the bomb goes off."

"You won't survive the blast," Katie said. "Please. Let us save you."

"No." Ethan stumbled through the water back to the shore. He scrambled up the bank.

"Ethan!"

He disappeared into the shadows. Mark yanked hard on the engine cord. It caught. The small engine roared to life, sending the tiny boat flying up the lake.

"Ethan... He just ran..." Katie collapsed onto the bench.

"I know."

"But he's going to...the place is going to..."

"I—" But he never got a chance to finish his thought. Because in that second a noise like the slamming of a heavy door exploded through the air around them. A spout of flames and smoke shot up through the trees. The air cracked. Fire fell down around them like rain.

Shielding his eyes, he held her tightly against him. The small boat sped away.

TWENTY-TWO

Mark edged the boat against the side of his island. Then he leaped out and tied the rope around a tree. They'd barely made it halfway across the lake when the engine had finally given up and died for good. He reached for her hand and helped her out.

"How long do you think until they find us?"

"Not long."

She curled her fingers through his. He led her up the rock to its peak. The sky above the clubhouse still burned red with fire.

But he turned her face to where a small cascade of lights twinkled gently against the night sky. "See those lights? That's the party." His arms slid around her waist. She leaned back into the warmth of his chest. "As you can see, the bombs they planted in the gala never went off. We did it."

She turned toward him, her body caught inside the circle of his arms. Static hissed from inside his pocket. "Mark? Are you there?"

"Albright!" He let her go. "When the broadcast

unit exploded, it must have stopped blocking the signal." He pulled the walkie-talkie from his pocket. "Yeah, I'm here."

"It's good to hear your voice. Our emergency crews are on their way to the explosion at the clubhouse."

"Katie and I are okay. We're on the island. Ethan Randall—" he took a deep breath "—didn't make it."

There was a pause on the other end of the phone. "I'm sorry to hear that. You might also be interested to know police have Allan Blau in custody. For some reason, he stumbled directly into your father's backyard. Your father insisted on handling it personally."

Katie hid a smile. "You told him which way to run?"

He nodded.

"Shall I send a boat for you?"

"Please. But first give us a few moments."

"Very well." Mark slid the walkie-talkie back into his pocket. He turned back to Katie. A grin spread across his face.

She could feel the corner of her lips turning up. "So what happens next?"

"How would you feel about flying to Lebanon with me?"

"Really? You're still jetting off across the globe tomorrow?"

"Well, maybe not tomorrow." His arms took back

their place around her body. His fingers stroked the small of her back. "I think I should spend a few days here first. Sort things out with Dad and Sunny—if she'll talk to me. Plus I've got to make sure TRUST and Nick are in good shape before I go. Reporters are sure to be swarming all over us, so I'm definitely going to need your help in preparing for that and figuring out how to come up with something coherent to say. I'm counting on you to save me from a media meltdown. So, maybe we fly next weekend?"

She laughed. "You're not worried at all about my safety traveling to the Middle East?"

"I'm more worried at the thought of my being anywhere without you. I need you there to remind me there's a life beyond my workshop table." His lips flitted gently over the line of her jaw. "I need someone to remind me of just how very much I need the touch of another human being. I need you with me."

She slid her hand up to his face and pushed him back. "Right now you need an ice pack. You have a pretty serious black eye." She tilted his head from one side to the other "No—make that two of them. And your mouth's seen better days too, I bet."

Mark chuckled. "I'm willing to risk it." He took her hand in his and pulled it away from his face. "You're no beauty queen yourself right now, babe," he said gruffly. "But so help me, I am so in love with you."

"I love you, too."

Then gently, carefully his lips found hers. Tentatively at first, kissing her lightly as if he was afraid she might disappear into the mist. Then growing stronger, wrapping his arms around her. He pulled her to him like a lifeline—with an intensity that took her breath away.

EPILOGUE

A warm June breeze drifted through the open window. Mark straightened his tie and ran his hand through his hair. At least he'd remembered to get a haircut. Of all the papers that had been signed and decisions that had been made since the formation of SHIELD-TRUST eight months ago, the importance of this one would eclipse them all.

There was a knock on the door. "Ready, son?" Jonah's head appeared around the corner.

"Just about."

His father nodded. "Your sister is here. Hiding in the back and threatening to walk."

Unexpected joy swept through Mark's heart. "But at least she's made a step toward reconciliation." He hadn't seen her since the day after the clubhouse exploded. While chaos still reigned and police swarmed the property, she'd walked into their father's cabin and handed him the signed legal papers she'd privately had drawn up and then left without saying a word. The fifty-fifty split of Jonah's legacy was done. She would buy out his half of the company for a fair price. He got financial freedom. Sunny got Shields Corp. He grinned. She'd done incredible things with the company—starting by building affordable housing communities.

"Now, come on." Jonah put a hand on his shoulder. "Believe me. Some things can't wait."

Mark swallowed hard and followed his father out into the sanctuary of a downtown Toronto church. He stood at the front between his father and Zack, willing his legs to stay still. His eyes swept the crowd. Then the back doors of the church opened, and he felt his world freeze.

Under the gaze of a simple lace veil, Katie's eyes met his. Trusting. Loving. His.

Peace swept through his heart as she walked up the aisle toward him, her wedding dress flowing out like waves on the beach.

Thank You, God, for this woman who pushes me and challenges me. Who has stepped down from her job to travel the world by my side and be my equal partner in founding our new charity. Who is now, today, willing to join me in reclaiming the tarnished Shields family name as our own, and, God willing, would help me raise a whole new generation of Shields who love the Lord, those in need and each other.

Katie stepped up beside him. Her fingers brushed against his. A smile lit her eyes.

Mark Shields held his bride's hand tightly as they turned toward the pastor, and he whispered, "Welcome to the adventure."

* * * * *

Dear Reader,

Just like Katie and Mark's journey, writing this book took some unexpected twists and turns for me. Years ago, I was working as a journalist overseas, visiting real-life heroes and heroines who are working to make a difference in our world. Their dedication inspired me, and snippets of Mark's experiences are based on their stories. Just like Katie, I wanted to stay in my job forever.

Then my life took an unexpected turn. We were blessed with two baby girls, after doctors had warned us to expect a life without children. I stepped down from globe-trotting, and we moved to a small community in Canada, where I juggled motherhood with interviewing those in my own backyard. While it hasn't always been easy, my life and my characters are richer for it.

Maybe your own story is not heading where you expected it to. Maybe you feel knocked off course, by changes in your job, family or relationships. I hope like Katie and Mark you'll be able to find comfort in the knowledge that nothing will take you out of God's sight. As the Bible reminds us, Jesus is the author of life. Every one of our days—

even the confusing and unexpected ones—is written in His book.

Thank you for sharing Mark and Katie's story with me.

Maggie

Questions for Discussion

1. Throughout the book, Katie trusts her instincts about people, and often makes quick decisions about them based on their appearance. What do you think of how Katie makes snap judgments about people? How do you think her first impression of Mark impacted the course of their relationship?

2. Have you ever had to make a decision about the honesty and trustworthiness of another person before you hired, listened to, or believed them? How did you make your decision? Were you right?

3. Both Katie and Mark enjoy helping other people, but find it hard to accept help from others. Why do you think they find it so difficult? Do you find it easier to offer help or accept it?

4. When Katie tried talking to people at church about her problems at work, she felt they didn't understand. If Katie had talked to you about her struggles with Ethan, what would you have told her?

5. Both Mark and Katie work very hard, but object to being called workaholics. What is your

definition of a workaholic? Do you think they are workaholics?

6. Several people in this book struggle to find balance in their lives. What advice would you give someone who works very hard at their job, volunteering or family obligations, but wants to find balance in their life? How do you maintain balance in your own life?

7. One of the reasons Katie stays in a job that makes her miserable is her fear of losing it. What changes her mind about her job? Why does she decide not to take the editorship in the end, after working so hard for it? Have you ever worked hard for a goal and then realized you no longer wanted it?

8. When thinking about his family, Mark reflects that loving someone is not the same as knowing how to get along with them. Do you think Mark was right to cut ties with his family when he launched his charity? If he had asked your advice before founding TRUST, how might you have advised him to handle the decision differently?

9. In Mark's story we can see reflections of the biblical parable of the prodigal son. But in Jesus's story, the son leaves home to party and waste

his money in wild living. Mark leaves home to do good in the world and to make a difference. How do Mark's motivations affect how people might view his decision?

10. How do you think Sunny's childhood has an impact on the way she treats her brother and father? Do you feel sympathy for her? Why or why not?

11. Did you find that Mark's decision to keep his full identity a secret from Katie was understandable? Did you agree with his reasons? When do you think he should have told her he was Jonah Shields's son? Why?

12. When Mark sees Jonah trimming the rosebushes he runs right past him without even recognizing him. Why do you think he didn't recognize his father? Do you think it was understandable?

13. Both Mark and Katie have some compassion for the teenagers Al has recruited, and express the hope that after being arrested, the teens will get the help they need to find a better way of life. What do you think it would take for someone like Billy to turn his life around?

14. What do you think Jonah's decision to split the company between his children says about him and his priorities? Do you agree with his de-

cision? Do you think he would have made the same decision before he found God? Why or why not?

15. Were you surprised when Mark and Sunny did not fully reconcile at the end of the book? What do you think will happen in their relationship going forward? What advice would you give each of them?

REQUEST YOUR FREE BOOKS!

2 FREE RIVETING INSPIRATIONAL NOVELS
PLUS 2 FREE MYSTERY GIFTS

YES! Please send me 2 FREE Love Inspired® Suspense novels and my 2 FREE mystery gifts (gifts are worth about $10). After receiving them, if I don't wish to receive any more books, I can return the shipping statement marked "cancel." If I don't cancel, I will receive 4 brand-new novels every month and be billed just $4.74 per book in the U.S. or $5.24 per book in Canada. That's a savings of at least 21% off the cover price. It's quite a bargain! Shipping and handling is just 50¢ per book in the U.S. and 75¢ per book in Canada.* I understand that accepting the 2 free books and gifts places me under no obligation to buy anything. I can always return a shipment and cancel at any time. Even if I never buy another book, the two free books and gifts are mine to keep forever.

123/323 IDN F5AN

Name	(PLEASE PRINT)	

Address		Apt. #

City	State/Prov.	Zip/Postal Code

Signature (if under 18, a parent or guardian must sign)

Mail to the **Harlequin® Reader Service:**
IN U.S.A.: P.O. Box 1867, Buffalo, NY 14240-1867
IN CANADA: P.O. Box 609, Fort Erie, Ontario L2A 5X3

**Are you a current subscriber to Love Inspired Suspense books
and want to receive the larger-print edition?
Call 1-800-873-8635 or visit www.ReaderService.com.**

* Terms and prices subject to change without notice. Prices do not include applicable taxes. Sales tax applicable in N.Y. Canadian residents will be charged applicable taxes. Offer not valid in Quebec. This offer is limited to one order per household. Not valid for current subscribers to Love Inspired Suspense books. All orders subject to credit approval. Credit or debit balances in a customer's account(s) may be offset by any other outstanding balance owed by or to the customer. Please allow 4 to 6 weeks for delivery. Offer available while quantities last.

Your Privacy—The Harlequin® Reader Service is committed to protecting your privacy. Our Privacy Policy is available online at www.ReaderService.com or upon request from the Harlequin Reader Service.
We make a portion of our mailing list available to reputable third parties that offer products we believe may interest you. If you prefer that we not exchange your name with third parties, or if you wish to clarify or modify your communication preferences, please visit us at www.ReaderService.com/consumerschoice or write to us at Harlequin Reader Service Preference Service, P.O. Box 9062, Buffalo, NY 14269. Include your complete name and address.

LISDIR13R